D0266169

MARIENBAD

MARIENBAD

Sholom Aleichem

translated by Aliza Shevrin

Weidenfeld and Nicolson
London

First published in Great Britain by
George Weidenfeld & Nicolson Limited
91 Clapham High Street, London SW4

ISBN 0 297 78200 2

Printed in Great Britain by
Redwood Burn Limited
Trowbridge

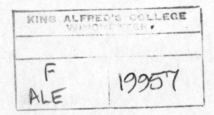

To my dearest husband, Howie,
with deepest love

MARIENBAD

TRANSLATOR'S INTRODUCTION

"Not a novel but an entanglement *[ferpluntenish]* between two cities: Warsaw and Marienbad, told through 36 letters, 14 love notes and 46 telegrams." In these words Sholom Aleichem prepares his reader for *Marienbad* on the title page of the Yiddish edition.

We are all familiar with the Sholom Aleichem who wrote the bittersweet chronicles depicting Jewish life in the *shtetl* of the 1880s. There he dealt with a group of small-town characters whose poverty and piety were for him and his readers an almost endless source of stories in which were described their struggles for a dignified survival.

Marienbad introduces an interesting change in Sholom Aleichem's subject matter. In *Marienbad*, he is dealing with middle-class, bourgeois businessmen, status-oriented, socially striving and competitive. These are well-off people with values different from those of the *shtetl* Jews. They are successful, urbane and eager to partake of the luxuries of life. Although they maintain their Jewish identities, customs, and some, if not all, of their religious observances, they scoff at their overly devout brethren whose wives take every opportunity to "cast off their wigs," the symbol

9

of their orthodoxy, as soon as they leave home to go abroad.

Marienbad was written in 1911, five years before the author's death, when he was in the process of emigrating to the United States. He was already dying of tuberculosis but the disease was in remission at various times between 1909 and 1913. For most of that time, although a semi-invalid, he spent blissful summers on the Italian Riviera and made several reading tours through Poland and Russia. He was also working on his autobiography, *From the Fair*, and wrote his railway stories and his novel, *Wandering Stars*. According to his granddaughter and translator, Tamara Kahana, he attended the Tenth Zionist Congress in Basel and was given a warm reception. This Congress figures in some of the events described in *Marienbad*.

The historical relationship between Jewish Warsaw and Marienbad began long before the events described in Sholom Aleichem's work. Jews had settled in Marienbad as far back as 1820. This German-speaking resort town in western Bohemia—part of the Austro-Hungarian Empire at the time the events in the novel took place and now part of Czechoslovakia—was sought out by Russian and Polish Jewry for its famous health-giving mineral waters. By 1884 Marienbad could boast of a synagogue. In 1938, during the Sudeten crisis, most of the Jewish community fled; those who remained were arrested by the Nazis. The synagogue was burned down; its site is now a park. In 1945 a Jewish community was reestablished and by 1949 it numbered 196 inhabitants. Sadly, the current center of Jewish life in Czech Marienbad is an old-age home with a chapel and a kosher restaurant frequented by its one hundred residents drawn from all parts of Czechoslovakia.

But in its Jewish heyday Marienbad was an elegant spa, beautifully located in the Bohemian hills, its centerpiece the Tempietto-style Kreutzbrunen, the fountain around which it was fashionable to stroll in order to show off one's latest social or sartorial acquisition. It provided many kosher restaurants for the more observant Jews, and there were secluded spots for trysting couples and lively cafés for those who wished to spend their leisure time watching the passing scene, reading newspapers or playing a game of Preference, Sixty-six, Okeh or Buntshak (popular card games of the early 1900s). Vacationers could make the rounds of several nearby spas when one or another place might have failed to provide them with eligible mates, satisfactory dalliances or luck at cards. To Marienbad came wives of busy merchants, mothers with marriageable daughters, fortune hunters, married men eager for romantic adventures—most of them, as Sholom Aleichem would have it, from the Nalevkis, named after Nalewki Street, a large east-west thoroughfare in the Jewish section of Warsaw, later to become the infamous Ghetto. Back home on the Nalevkis were the merchants too busy to take time off and the forsaken wives. The stage was thus set for the inevitable entanglements told through letters, love notes and telegrams.

Marienbad was not the first work in which Sholom Aleichem used the epistolary form of the novel first

11

introduced by Samuel Richardson in the eighteenth century. Sholom Aleichem's *Menachem Mendl*, published in 1892, was entirely based on an exchange of letters between Menachem Mendl, the archetypical *luftmensh*, and his wife, Sheyne Sheyndl. While *Menachem Mendl* is essentially a dialogue, *Marienbad* has many voices. The letters seethe with intrigue, gossip and remonstrations of love. The convention of the interior monologue, used so successfully by Sholom Aleichem in such well-known works as *Tevye the Dairyman*, and *Mottel the Cantor's Son*, is in *Marienbad* transformed into direct communication between one character and another, which still provides Sholom Aleichem the opportunity to demonstrate his uncanny knack of depicting character through speech while exercising his virtuosity in exploiting the remarkable responsiveness of the Yiddish language to feeling, personal circumstance, social status and education. Each letter is thus an interior monologue which reveals the writer's character and condition while advancing the plot and revealing the writer's attitude toward the recipient of the communication.

Only a Sholom Aleichem could pull this all off to such comic effect. With a turn of phrase or an idiom, he can bring a character to life. Fawning friends become mortal enemies as the gossip flies through the mails. Secrets are exposed, confidences betrayed, marriages ruined, others cemented, and "charlatans" have a heyday.

I can imagine the knowledgeable Jewish reader of Yiddish in Sholom Aleichem's day literally rolling on

12

the floor with laughter as he recognized each refer-
ence to a particular social group or a play on words
alluding to some current event. Sholom Aleichem's
rendering of the various dialects, mispronunciations
and Talmudic misquotes (not as extensive as Tevye's
but humorous nonetheless) must have been very
familiar to his reading public. It brings to mind the
enjoyment Gilbert and Sullivan must have provided
to the Londoners of their day, who were acutely
aware of all the topical allusions as well as the targets
of their satires. And yet, we who hear Gilbert and
Sullivan today without being aware of all these
ramifications can heartily enjoy and appreciate their
universality and good humor. Similarly, Sholom
Aleichem was satirizing the late nineteenth and early
twentieth century institutions and mores of high-
flown German Jews, pretentious Russian Jews, hypo-
critical Orthodox Jews, nouveau riche businessmen
and their upwardly mobile wives. It was his special
genius that he was able to capture the nuances of
speech of each Yiddish dialect with all of its social
implications. Often these dialects differed in the
degree to which they incorporated elements of neigh-
boring languages such as Russian, Polish and German. In addition, individual speakers used these
other languages to convey nuances of meaning,
educational level, degree of assimilation, one-upman-
ship, etcetera. And over and above Russian, Polish
and German, there was always Hebrew, the holy
tongue, which was often put to unholy and quite
secular uses.

For the translator, these rich linguistic resources

drawn upon by Sholom Aleichem constitute the supreme challenge and nightmare. Not only is there the usual task of knowing the meaning of the Yiddish even when it contains words not included in the dictionaries, and not only must the translator find the equivalent meaning or idiom in English appropriate to the character, but the translator must also succeed in conveying the influence of *third* languages in both their denotative and connotative meanings. It would be like translating into French a conversation between an American Southerner and an Irishman, with the latter throwing in some Gaelic for good measure.

I have tried to solve this knotty translating problem by inventing stylistic signatures. For example, Meyer'l Mariomchik, the Odesser Womanizer, writes in a Yiddish that can be understood only by one who knows Russian as well. He writes absolutely bilingually, conjugating Russian words according to Yiddish grammatical rules. *Spletnitze* is used to mean a gossip, *oshibaye* is to enjoy, and so forth. I have attempted to convey this by making his English include a few "foreign" elements. Shlomo Kurlander uses a Hebrew word even when a Yiddish word would suffice, perhaps to show off a bit, while Velvel Yamayiker uses Yiddish and Hebrew equally, as Meyer'l does with the Russian: *Dyne michtov* (Hebrew) *hob ich m'kabl* (Hebrew) *geven*, means "I got your letter." I tried to show his stuffiness and formality by translating it "I am in receipt of your letter." Chaim Soroker is garrulous and loves to embroider his Yiddish with elaborate details in an attempt to show how good a writer he is. A more expansive English vocabulary is used for his letters. Hirsh Loiferman writes in an authentic, lower-class Warsaw dialect in which the vowels are drawn out as in an American Southern accent. A simpler syntax and vocabulary are provided for him. Svirsky, the international matchmaker, prefers a Yiddish full of German until he becomes enraged at being cheated, and then he lapses completely into his mother tongue, Yiddish, the most expressive language in the world for cursing. The Germanic Yiddish is rendered in an inflated English and his abusive Yiddish in more basic Anglo-Saxon. A special note must be made of Itzhak-Meyer Sherentzis and Itzhak-Meyer Pekelis, the two Orthodox husbands in Warsaw. Their nickname, Itche-Meyer, is a derogatory colloquialism for dunce or oaf (e.g., "What a dumb *Itche-Meyer* he is!). These two, so steeped in the Bible and the Talmud, first write their long letter in Hebrew and then translate it into a Yiddish that still retains a Biblical sound and style. In order to capture this quality, I have translated their letter into a Biblical, prayerbook English.

The women, by contrast, do not present the same difficulties to the translator. For the most part, the women write a purer, more direct and pragmatic Yiddish than the men, more colloquial and much less infiltrated with Hebrew and other languages. Perhaps this is so because the women were not permitted a religious education, nor did they have the same opportunities as the men to mingle with non-Jewish speakers. On the other hand, their Yiddish reveals much more subtle variations in tone in order to express differences in age and personality. Keep in mind that unlike a standard piece of fiction, this one has no narrator or "thinking mind" to provide us with descriptions or motives. The young Beltzi Kurlander, our heroine, writes in a breathless, headlong Yiddish that is vivid and personal. The older gossip, Madam Yamayichke, clearly has not mastered the difference between writing and speaking, so her sentences run on repeatedly and insistently.

There are problems in translation posed by the structure of the Yiddish language itself and the availability of words to convey certain universal meanings. It is rich in exhortations to God, in insults and in descriptions of poverty and tragedy. In Yiddish we find the increasingly emphatic expressions *chalila*, *chas v'chalila*, and *chas v'sholom*. All these can best be translated by only one phrase: "God forbid"—or perhaps an old-fashioned person might use "Heaven forfend." But this paucity is more than compensated for by the abundant choices we are given for the Yiddish word *shayn*. We can choose from "nice," "pretty," "handsome," "lovely," "good," "delicious," "fine," "well" and "beautiful," at the very least. I will leave the understanding of this fact to linguists.

There was the minor problem of finding just the right qualifier for Meyer'l Mariomchik's name. In Yiddish, Sholom Aleichem calls him Meyer'l "Charlatan." Roget offers as synonyms for the word "charlatan" such possibilities as "hooligan," "cad," "imposter," "fraud," "mountebank," "phony," "faker," "cheat," "quack" and "bounder." In the book

16

he is really none of these, but a ladies' man, a flirt. I could have called him Meyer'l Don Juan or Romeo or Casanova. I decided on Womanizer and hope it will serve to describe him, as well as having a more modern and appropriate sound. Every reader of Yiddish will justifiably feel that some particular idiom might have been translated differently or better, and I would agree. I can only state that I have been meticulous in translating every nuance, every phrase and every idiom.

In closing, I would like to suggest that *Marienbad* is an important and challenging work which occupies a special place in the author's literary corpus. Oddly, it has not been published in translation before, as far as I know, nor are there any references to it in scholarly bibliographies, critiques and accounts of Sholom Aleichem's output. In *Marienbad* Sholom Aleichem portrays the totally vanished life of middle-class urban Jews in the Poland prior to World War One. The value of this work lies in its unique representation of a people who always existed in an isolated and dissident relationship to the surrounding dominant culture. In this important respect Eastern European Jewry reflected in its daily experience what has since come to be appreciated as the plight of minority and Third World cultures in our own day. What is noteworthy is the tenacity with which they struggled to maintain their ethnic identity in the face of powerful examples of an entirely different way of life. It took the madmen of the Third Reich to destroy them.

The Nalevkis of Warsaw and its lively existence is

17

no more. The Polish Jewish community is no more. Jewish Marienbad is no more. It is my hope that the availability of this translation will provide the world with a record, albeit fictional, of a vital and vibrant community, of people who led interesting lives relatively free from prejudice and want. Only God knows, and we can try to imagine, how different the world and the Jewish people might have been had the Jews of such communities been allowed to live.

I wish to express my gratitude to the members of my family, friends and scholars whose suggestions, advice, encouragement and expertise have been of great help to me in completing this project. I am thankful to my beloved parents, Rabbi Eliezer and Rivka Goldberger, who were constant sources of knowledge and support. My friend Joan W. Blos, the distinguished writer, is an inspiration upon whom I draw daily. I am grateful for the kind support of Bel Kaufman, noted writer and granddaughter of Sholom Aleichem. I wish also to thank Anya Finkel and Menasha Feldstein for their assistance in translating the Russian words, Rabbi Allen D. Kensky for his help with Biblical Hebrew, Professors Zvi Gitelman and Yehuda Reinharz for making their wide-ranging knowledge of Jewish history and culture available to me, and Dorothy Foster, my wonderful typist.

My husband, to whom I dedicate this translation, has been a vital contributor to my Yiddish translating efforts for almost twenty years. His love of language, his appreciation of the ways human beings express themselves, his sharp, critical mind and generosity of spirit have been abundantly available to me. He is my indispensable "second set of ears." I am deeply grateful to him and very lucky to have his invaluable collaboration.

Aliza Shevrin
Ann Arbor, Michigan
February 1982

Characters in the Novel

In Marienbad

Beltzi Kurlander, young second wife of Shlomo Kurlander

Chaim Soroker, husband of Esther Soroker

Chava'le (Chava, Eva) Tchopnik, wife of Berel Tchopnik, cousin of Beltzi Kurlander

Pearl Yamayiker (the Yamayichke), wife of Velvel Yamayiker

The Three Noses, eligible daughters of the Yamayikers

On the Nalevkis in Warsaw

Shlomo (Solomon) Kurlander, elderly husband of Beltzi

Esther Soroker, wife of Chaim, sister of Chan'tzi

Berel (Bernard) Tchopnik, husband of Chava'le

Velvel (Volf) Yamayiker, husband of the Yamayichke

In Marienbad	On the Nalevkis in Warsaw
Meyer'l (Meyer, Mark) Mariomchik, known as the Odesser Womanizer, husband of Chan'tzi Mariomchik, brother-in-law of Chaim Soroker, cousin of Pearl Yamayiker	Chan'tzi (Chana, Anna) Mariomchik, wife of Meyer'l, sister of Esther Soroker
Broni Loiferman, wife of Hirsh Loiferman	Hirsh (Tzvi) Loiferman, husband of Broni, winner of lottery
Leah'tzi (Leah) Broichshtul, wife of Kalman Broichshtul	Kalman Broichshtul, husband of Leah'tzi
Sheintzi Sherentzis, wife of Itche-Meyer Sherentzis	Itzhak Meyer (Itche-Meyer) Sherentzis, husband of Sheintzi
Kreintzi Pekelis, wife of Itche-Meyer Pekelis	Itzhak Meyer (Itche-Meyer) Pekelis, husband of Kreintzi Pekelis
Alexander Svirsky, international matchmaker	

In Marienbad	*In Odessa*
Alfred Zeidener, dentist from Kishinev	David Mariomchik, father of Meyer'l Mariomchik
Rebecca Zeidener, wife of Alfred Zeidener	

1.

*Beltzi Kurlander from Berlin to her husband,
Shlomo Kurlander, on the Nalevkis in
Warsaw.*

To my dear husband the learned Shlomo may his
light shine forever.

I want to let you know that I am still in Berlin. I
am hoping to be able to leave for Marienbad after
Shabbes. I really don't owe you any explanation.
You must believe me that it's not my fault I've had
to stay on an extra whole week. When you hear
what I've been through, you will have to agree that
it's never possible to figure things out beforehand.
As they say, "Man proposes and God disposes."
  I had counted on spending one day or two days at
most in Berlin. How long should it take to see a
specialist? It might have worked out if *he* had come
to see *me*. But I thought to myself, Why should I
make you spend an extra thirty marks which can
come in handy for something else? You are always
reminding me that we spend too much money. The
times, you insist, are not the best—you go on and
on. Maybe that's why I didn't want to stay at that

25

hotel on Friedrichstrasse where my cousin Chava'le made reservations for me. How can I compare myself to Chava'le Tchopnik? Chava'le can spend as much as she likes and no one will complain because Chava'le isn't her husband's second wife, as I am, and her husband doesn't have any children from his first wife, as my husband has, and Berel Tchopnik doesn't tremble over every groschen, as you do, and he isn't afraid to remain a pauper in his old age, as you are. I don't mean, God forbid, to say anything against you, but I tell you frankly that I hate to run up extra expenses. So that is why I decided to stay at a place where many of our Nalevkis friends stay, at Madam Perelzweig's. The woman is a widow, a very capable person and an honest one. She is a good cook, charges reasonable prices, and her place is not far from everything. For just ten pfennigs you are on Leipzigerstrasse, at Wertheimer's. And how is it possible to be in Berlin and not step into Wertheimer's for a minute? If you would see Wertheimer's just once, you would say that it is not to be believed. I had already heard of Wertheimer's back in Warsaw, but never did I imagine that on this earth there could be such a store. What can I tell you, my dear husband? It can't be put into words! You can't see enough, you can't say enough! And people! The mobs—so packed together you couldn't squeeze in a fingernail. And everything dirt-cheap, exactly half of what we have to pay on the Nalevkis. Just picture it—two marks for a dozen handkerchiefs! Or for ninety-eight pfennigs you can get a pair of silk stockings that you can't buy for a

ruble and twenty in Warsaw. Or, for instance, a
wall clock for sixty-eight pfennigs—tell me, is it
possible? I figure that with God's help, when I am
all better, on my way home I will return through
Berlin, not Vienna—Vienna is, they say, a
provincial town, a nothing compared to Berlin—and
then I will really be able to spend some time at
Wertheimer's and, with a clear head, do some
serious shopping for the house—some glassware,
some faience and other household articles, some silk
goods, furniture and perfumes. Don't worry at all
about customs; I'll manage somehow. Chava'le
Tchopnik brings over whole cratefuls every year. In
the meantime, I've hardly bought anything except
some underwear, a pair of summer shoes, a little
hat, a nightgown made entirely of ribbon, a half-
dozen petticoats, a green umbrella, handkerchiefs
and a few odds and ends which I must have for
Marienbad. And while I was already at
Wertheimer's, I couldn't resist the excellent buys
and asked them to pack in a half-dozen tablecloths,
two dozen napkins and a special machine for making
butter. I could kick myself for not listening to you
and taking along an extra few hundred rubles. It was
so stupid of me to want to show off to you that I am
not as big a spendthrift as you think. Better to
spend it at Wertheimer's than on that doctor, may
he suffer for it! Just what I needed in Berlin—a
doctor! As if we don't have enough of them in
Warsaw. You can bet the Berlin doctors would have
to wait a long time before I would send for them.
But fate had to arrange a misfortune. Just listen.

27

I had barely arrived at the lodgings—at Perelzweig's, as I told you. Even before I had had a chance to change or wash up properly, I was immediately asked the question—what kind of doctor do I want called in? So I said, "First of all, who told you that I need a doctor? Am I so sick that you can see it on my face? And second of all," I said, "I have brought with me from back home the address of a specialist." Then this old bachelor, a man with red pimples on his nose, spoke up. "Don't be offended, Madam," said he, "at what I will tell you. It's *because*," said he, "you have the address of a specialist that you must first see," said he, "a regular doctor. Because there's a big difference," said he, "between what *you* would tell the specialist and," said he, "what the *doctor* would tell him in his doctor's language." It turns out that this old bachelor with the red nose actually lives at the widow Perelzweig's, whom I told you about, and he arranges appointments with doctors. That means his job is to get a doctor if you need one and then the doctor gets the specialist or he even takes you to the specialist's office himself. So I politely let him know that nobody was taking me anywhere. "I am still," said I, "thank God, strong enough to walk a mile." So this doctor-arranger with the red pimples retorted, "Madam! As far as I'm concerned," said he, "you can walk three miles. But I must tell you ahead of time that you're wasting your time. If you visit a Berlin specialist on your own," said he, "without first seeing a regular doctor, then the specialist won't spend so much as half a minute with you," said he, "*fee-foo-fah*, a poke with the finger, one-two-three and out you go! Finished! But if you come," said he, "with your *own* doctor, then it's another story. A doctor he can't refuse; a doctor he has to listen to. Have you gotten the point yet," said he, "or not?"

To make a long story short, he called in a doctor for me. Right off, he didn't appeal to me. He didn't look me in the eye, he didn't have enough time for me, and he spoke in a squeaky voice. Would you like a doctor who doesn't look you in the eye and talks with a squeak?

First he questioned me thoroughly—who and what and when—and examined me all over. Then he insisted, this smart doctor, that I stay in bed till the following day when he would, said he, examine me again and then he would tell me, you see, which kind of a specialist he would refer me to. When I heard that he wanted to confine me to my bed, I let him know in no uncertain terms that he should forget about anything like that. "I didn't come," said I, "to Berlin to lie in bed. I have to go," said I, "to shop at Wertheimer's and at Teitz's and furthermore, I want," said I, "to go everywhere. If you wish," said I, "to come tomorrow, you are welcome, but for me to stay in bed—that," said I, "won't do!" He thought he had found himself some dummy from the Nalevkis from whom he could make a fortune. I could tell right away this was no doctor but a leech. As proof, just listen to what this bloodsucker did. It makes my hair stand on end!

In the morning, the two of us went to see the

specialist and it turned out that it wasn't at all the specialist that Chava'le Tchopnik had told me about but another specialist for completely different ailments. This I discovered only after I had been put through torture and we were on our way home. That is, I *thought* we were going back home. It turns out we were going to yet another specialist and still not to the one I had in mind. This time he brought me to a woman's specialist! So I became quite properly indignant and started to make a fuss. The doctor then scolded me in his squeaky voice, I should remember that I wasn't in Warsaw on the Nalevkis but in Berlin and that I shouldn't make such a fuss and that he had no time and that he knew better than I what kind of specialist I needed. How can you argue with that? And so, as I'm telling you, we visited, if you can believe it, three specialists, and all three specialists, as if they had agreed ahead of time, said the same thing, "Marienbad!" So tell me, did I need three specialists to tell me that? Marienbad I had already heard about in Warsaw. In short, a waste of time, a waste of money. But what's done is done.

I went back to my lodgings so exhausted that I could barely stand on my feet. I simply had to lie down. Do you think I was allowed to rest for long? That doctor should only live as long as I rested! You can't imagine the bill I was presented with by this highway robber. I jumped out of bed as if struck by a thunderbolt. I should pay him, said he, eighty marks! Why eighty marks? "A simple addition," said he. "Two visits at ten marks each—is twenty. Three

30

consultations with three specialists at twenty apiece—is sixty. Sixty and twenty are," said he, "always and everywhere, eighty." I must have made such an uproar that the whole house came running: the widowed landlady, the old bachelor—that *shlimazel*—and all the other guests. "Where are we?" I screamed at them, "In Berlin or Sodom? It's a thousand times worse here," said I, "than it is in Russia! You don't have doctors here, but hooligans! *Pogromchiks!*" I tell you, whatever came into my head, that's what I said to them. Try to picture the scene—people came crowding around us, and finally, finally they worked it out between us so that I would only have to pay him fifty-five marks. Fifty-five boils should fester on his face, that fine doctor! Do you think I'm finished? Hold on. Remember there's still that old bachelor with the red nose and the pimples. *He* wants fifteen marks too. What for? "That," said he, "is my commission for recommending the doctor." What do you say to such a lout? This made my blood boil so that it brought on my old symptoms and I had to take to bed with a migraine till the following day. It's no small matter—to throw out so much money and, I ask you, for what? For whom? Wouldn't it have been ten thousand times better to have spent it at Wertheimer's? I'm eating myself up alive for not coming here a week earlier. I would have been with my cousin Chava'le—a relative, after all, and I wouldn't have fallen into the hands of these leeches. It's just lucky that Berlin is a city in which there is a great deal to see or else I would die of boredom.

31

You can see more in Berlin in one day than you can see in thirty years in Warsaw. In addition to Wertheimer's and Teitz's and other big stores, there is a Wintergarden and an Apollo Theater and a Schumann Circus and a Busch Circus. They even say there is a Luna Park that's not to be described! I'm planning to go there, God willing, in the morning, so I'll write you about it in my letter tomorrow.

Meanwhile, be well and tell Sheva-Rochel to take care of things—not only the kitchen but the rest of the house as well. Before leaving I forgot to write down on the laundry list a little collar and two pillowcases. Also I opened a jar of jam the day I left. She should use that one for cooking and not dare to touch the jams on the balcony under the chest. And remember to write me, for God's sake, in Marienbad, Poste Restante, as we agreed.

From me, your wife,
Beltzi Kurlander

2.

*Shlomo Kurlander from the Nalevkis in
Warsaw to his friend Chaim Soroker in
Marienbad.*

My dear friend Chaim,

I must ask you, my dear friend, for a small favor.
It's really not a small favor. In fact, it is a big one.
A very big one. Something awful has happened to
me—my dear friend, my Beltzi must go to
Marienbad. Why suddenly to Marienbad? Ask me
something easier. She says she's not well and has to
go to Marienbad. And the doctor also says she's not
well and must go to Marienbad. Well, if two say a
third is drunk, then the third starts to feel
dizzy. . . . But confidentially, I'll tell you—between
the two of us, and I beg you to let it remain that
way—*I* understand what's behind Marienbad. If
Madam Tchopnik goes to Marienbad, why shouldn't
Madam Kurlander also go to Marienbad? She
compares me to Berel Tchopnik! She doesn't know,
apparently, that what Tchopnik can afford *I* can't
afford, *you* can't afford, *no one* can afford. Tchopnik
can sit around an entire year in the finest apartment
like a king and forget altogether that for an
apartment you have to pay rent. I remember the
time when Tchopnik rented one of my apartments. I

thought I would have apoplexy. Every day he would demand new repairs and he would order me around like a janitor. Anyone else I would have thrown out on his ear but because of Beltzi I had to take a bellyful from him and be silent. How come? Because his Chava'le and my Beltzi are third cousins, you know, a grandmother's sister's granddaughter. Really close relations! What I had to put up with that year from Berel Tchopnik would take a week to tell. When a butcher would come to collect, Berel Tchopnik wouldn't open the door more than a crack, shouting, "The nerve of a butcher to come asking for money!" And Madam Tchopnik, when you would try to present *her* with a bill, you'd wear out two pairs of shoes trying to collect, and after a while you'd quit trying. When it comes to tailors and shoemakers—forget about it. They already know you don't go to them to collect because you won't get anything. Need I say more? Just recently they gave a dinner party on the occasion of Madam Tchopnik's birthday, just before they left for Marienbad. Well, you should have seen what went on! I wasn't there, but my Beltzi told me that it was such a big spread it was enough to marry off two daughters. The food was catered by Hekselman's Restaurant and the meal was fit for a king: fish and meat and roasts and wine and beer and whatever your heart desired. Wineglasses were clinking, the servants were running about, it was lively. They played a game in which Tchopnik was banker, of course. Somehow, he always manages to come out on top; he knows how to work it. According to my

Beltzi there were hundreds in the kitty.
Nevertheless, when Hekselman came the following
morning to collect, they heaped such ridicule on his
head that he's still ashamed to talk about it. But I
got carried away talking about Tchopnik and almost
forgot my request.

My request is simply this: Since my Beltzi is
traveling to another country for the first time in her
life—she can't even open a door for herself and
doesn't know the language—I was wondering if you
would be so kind and help her out, recommend a
good lodging, a good doctor, a kosher restaurant—in
a word, be her guide. By the way, I'd also like to
ask you to keep an eye on her, see whom she meets
there and with whom she socializes. I want, you
understand, that she should keep some distance from
Madam Tchopnik. You might wonder what I have
against Madam Tchopnik. She's never hurt me. I
just don't want my Beltzi to be too cozy with
Madam Tchopnik, even though they *are* third
cousins. I don't want her to be a model for Beltzi, so
that whatever Madam Tchopnik says is good and
whatever Madam Tchopnik wears is pretty and
whatever Madam Tchopnik does my Beltzi will also
want to do. Believe me, dear friend, it's not the
money that matters to me. You know that I'm not,
God forbid, a miser. My Beltzi gets her way with
me, whatever she wants. She is, after all, a second
wife, and a second wife, they say, like an only
daughter, gets her way in everything. So you must
wonder what the problem is? I don't want my wife
to follow the crowd. Is that so terrible? I have, as it

35

is, enough enemies on the Nalevkis who would be happy to drown me in a teaspoon of water. And especially since I married Beltzi, they'd like to avenge themselves on me, don't ask me why. It's as if I was ruining someone's reputation or business. They say she's young enough to be my daughter-in-law. Why should that bother them? Troublemakers have already tried to stir up fights between us. I ask, what have I done to them? All this fuss because she's pretty. To hell with all of them. Would they have been happier if I had remarried an ugly woman?

And so, dear friend, I don't have to say anything more, you understand what I mean. I want you to keep an eye on her and to write me a letter occasionally telling me how you are and what you are doing and how Beltzi is and what she is doing. If she should come to you for money—I gave her your address—give her on my account whatever she asks—naturally, not all at once, but a little at a time—because money to her, just between us, has no value. I knew beforehand that if I gave her too much money to take along, as soon as she got to Berlin it would probably disappear into thin air. And it was just as I predicted. I've already received a letter from Berlin (on the way to Marienbad she stopped in Berlin), sending me regards from someone by the name of Wertheimer who owns some kind of store, this Wertheimer, where you can find, she says, even "bird's milk." She's already been there, she writes, and she gives me to understand that this Wertheimer wasn't disappointed in her.

She compares herself to Madam Tchopnik. Berel Tchopnik boasts that when his Chava'le went abroad, he gave her five hundred for the trip and when she arrived in Berlin she already wrote for more money and he had to send her another five hundred the following week. He throws five hundreds around, this Tchopnik! Do you have any idea what he does for a living? This man has been living in Warsaw for twenty years and I dare you to find anyone who can tell me what Berel Tchopnik's business is. He is a natty dresser with a prosperous paunch and a fancy accent who won't say one word more than is necessary. While he's looking at you, he is thinking how to trick you into lending him money he'll never repay.

In a word, this Tchopnik isn't worth the time spent talking about him. Again, I beg you, Chaim, you know how much my Beltzi means to me. I'm very disturbed that she's traveling alone. I would accompany her but how can I abandon my business? It's the height of the season. I'm putting up a few buildings and, God willing, in about a year I imagine I will be doing all right. As I see it, apartment houses should be making more money this year than last. But my Beltzi doesn't need to know this. Rather, if you have the opportunity, you can tell her the opposite—I don't need to teach you what to say; you already know. There's no other news. You get our newspapers there so you probably know that things are not going too well here. I can give you news of your Esther. I saw her from a distance and she looks as if she's about to give birth any day now. If it's a boy, how can there be a *bris* without you? So see to it, my friend, that you do what I ask and answer me soon.

From me, your best friend,
Shlomo Kurlander

3.

Beltzi Kurlander from Berlin to her husband, Shlomo Kurlander, on the Nalevkis in Warsaw.

To my dear husband the learned Shlomo may his light shine forever.

I promised you yesterday that I would describe the Berlin Luna Park as soon as I got back from there, so I am doing it for you even though it's an impossible task. If I sat here and wrote all night I would not be able to convey one tenth of what you can see in that Luna Park. Now, that's really some place! Picture in your mind a huge park ablaze with light wherever you look. Every building is lit up from top to bottom. As soon as you arrive, you step right into a Funny House. Once you enter this special hall you are completely overcome by laughter. You laugh so long and hard that you come close to bursting. Wherever you turn, you see your own face in the weirdest shapes. Then after buying a ticket you sit down in this silly train which flies crazily uphill and downhill. One minute it lifts you up above the houses, the next minute it hurls you down, down into hell itself till you feel you are about to explode. People start shrieking and screaming. Up it goes again taking you high up a hill and then *zoom!* down you go again toward the ground, till you return to where you started from and come to a stop, feeling like an idiot. The German ticket-taker tells you to step out and you do, totally bewildered. Then you come to a lake and you see people sliding downhill in these little boats. They dive straight into the water and don't drown! You get the urge to try it and climb up the steps to the top. You buy another ticket and sit down in a little boat and down you go like a lunatic right into the water. You get out of there soaking wet wondering why a German would ask you to pay for this. From there a little further on you see these wild dark gypsies from Egypt who dance and sing, leap and tumble, lick red-hot irons with their tongues, stab themselves with swords and wiggle their bellies. And for this they make you pay! They will take you, if you want, right into Gehenem itself where they show you corpses, devils and ghosts, snakes, scorpions and other hideous things. You think God to get out of there alive! Cafés, restaurants, cabarets, music boxes, movies, sideshows, photographs and more—they are as plentiful as the stars in the sky. If you let yourself go and take whatever these Germans offer you, you can come out of there more dead than alive. The whole thing, all in all, didn't cost me a single pfennig. How is that possible, you'll ask? You'll really like this.

Remember that bachelor, that lout with the pimples who gouged fifteen marks out of me for recommending that "fine" doctor? It was he who took me to Luna Park at his expense. He also treated me to Seltzer water, chocolate and whatever I wanted. I suppose he realized this made me feel ill at ease and he said to me, "For pretty young women who need a doctor, I am," said he, "an arranger. But to see Berlin, I am," said he, "no longer an arranger but a cavalier and a gentleman." What do you say to such a *shlimazel*? On the way back he said to me, this smart aleck, his face lighting up like the sun in July, "Madam! If you promise you won't be offended, I would like to tell you something." Said I, "Only if it's something clever." Said he, "I don't know if it's clever," said he, "but it will certainly be interesting to you." Said I, "If it's interesting, why not?" Said he, "Only on the condition, Madam, that you give me your reaction afterward." Said I, "Why shouldn't I?" Said he, "No, I mean I want you to be frank and not put me off." Said I, "Why should I put you off?" Said he, "No, I mean, if you don't like what I have to say," said he, "I want you to say so." Said I, "So talk. Stop pestering me like this." He stopped walking and this is what he said: "Listen, Madam, this is the way it is. Will you believe me or not? Maybe you'll believe me and maybe not, although I don't know why you shouldn't believe me. I am," said he, "a sincere person and what I have to say," said he, "I say. I hate," said he, "being wishy-washy. I come right out with it, one-two-three and it's over. I have to tell you, Madam," said he, "that I am the kind of person who, if I have something to say, I say it right out. I can't hold it in too long. I have wanted to tell you for a long time," said he, "that I have found you very attractive," said he, "from the moment," said he, "that I first saw you. What do you say," said he, "to that?" "What," said I, "can I say? You're lucky," said I, "that we're in Berlin on the Friedrichstrasse. Otherwise, I would show you," said I, "what I think of fresh men like you!" With that, our conversation ended right on the spot. From then on I remained without an escort and have had to go everywhere alone. But it's no problem. Berlin is not a wilderness and the Germans are the kind of people who are willing to stop and listen to you, show you the way and answer your questions. On the contrary, if you ask them something they don't know, you can see that it really irks them. A German remains a German.

So I've written you all that I promised. God willing, when I arrive safely in Marienbad, I will write you more news from there. Meanwhile, be well and be sure to keep me up on all the Warsaw news when I'm in Marienbad. How is Esther Soroker? Has she given birth yet? And if so, what did she have, a boy or a girl? Some devoted husband she has, I mean, Chaim Soroker—to leave a wife

41

when her baby is due and go off to Marienbad. Whoever heard of such a thing? He's the one who wants to "give birth," by losing that fat belly of his. If it were me, I'd never let him come back to the Nalevkis. I would make him stay in Marienbad forever. I would make him "give birth," all right, but it wouldn't be just his belly he would lose. Say what you like—I know he's a good friend of yours— but that's not the way to behave. It broke my heart when I went over to say goodbye to her. She's not the type to complain, but you could tell. They have the worst luck, those two sisters, both Esther and Chan'tzi. Chan'tzi, they say, is treated even worse by her Meyer. They told me here in Berlin that Meyer Mariomchik is also in Marienbad. And Broni Loiferman and Leah'tzi Broichshtul and Madam Yamayichke with her daughters are already in Marienbad. All of Nalevkis is in Marienbad. Not bad. I hope to find letters from you in Marienbad. Just don't forget to write what's doing at home. Don't leave everything to Sheva-Rochel. You should check every day on what she brings from the market and be sure to reweigh the meat she gets from the butcher and, for God's sake, pay cash for everything because even the most honest shopkeeper will add on a bit if you charge it. And if Leah, the dressmaker, comes to you complaining that I didn't pay her enough for her work and appeals to your good nature, don't you dare fall for it. She's threatened to take me to court. Let her try! And don't forget, I beg you, to send me money in

Marienbad. I'll send you my address as soon as I get there. I'm praying to God to arrive safely.

From me, your wife,
Beltzi Kurlander

4.

Shlomo Kurlander from the Nalevkis in Warsaw to his wife, Beltzi Kurlander, in Marienbad.

To my dear wife, Beltzi, long may she live.

I received both your letters from Berlin and can tell you, dear Beltzi, that I am, thank God, well and that everything is all right at home. I just wish the tenants would pay their rent on time so that I wouldn't have to sue them. Besides losing the rent money, there are expenses, lawyers, papers and other complications. And to make matters worse, there is the indignity I would suffer because some of these ingrates threaten to "expose" me in the newspapers if I evict them and I don't want to have my name in the papers. I hate it. These days the construction business eats up so much money that I don't know how I will ever break even. On top of that I have to deal with craftsmen and laborers, who talk back to me and have no respect for a boss. In short, what can I tell you, Beltzi dear? One trouble leads to two others. And then your letters arrive from Berlin. You can't possibly imagine how sorry I am that you didn't go to Vienna instead of to Berlin. Oh, well, I suppose you wanted a specialist's diagnosis. All right. I would never stop you and you know I would never scrimp on any amount of money when it comes to your health or welfare. It's bad enough to get entangled with those bloodsuckers and to need three specialists who will confuse you so that in the long run *they* will make you sick, but, I ask you, Beltzi dear, how can you risk your health by running around to Wertheimer's and Teitz's looking for bargains? I believe you when you say everything is half price, but your health is far more important, and besides you can get those same bargains in Warsaw. As they say, "For money you can get everything." Is it really a good idea to be pushed around in crowds? So you'll buy a few pairs of stockings and a wall clock—do you have to jeopardize your life for it? I ask you, Beltzi, you're not one of those Nalevkis *yentas*, so how come you did such a foolish thing? And to run around all over Berlin—I must say, Beltzi dear, I can't begin to understand what there is to see in Berlin. I picture a big city, three times, five times, ten times as big as Warsaw with nicer, taller buildings, a great deal nicer, a great deal taller. So what's so wonderful about that? Or, as you write, you went to the theater and the circus and other such places—that

doesn't bother me. Quite the opposite—when you
are in a foreign country you have to go everywhere
and see everything. Why not? But one thing *does*
bother me—that you jeopardize your own reputation
and status by allowing yourself to be led around by
any loafer whom you neither know nor should want
to know. It's a good thing the idiot respected you.
What would you have done if you had met a
hooligan or a scoundrel? In strange places, Beltzi,
you have to be even more cautious than at home.
The worst embarrassment or misfortune might
happen, God forbid. For this reason, I've written a
letter to my good friend Chaim Soroker, in
Marienbad, asking him to be available to you
occasionally for advice or a little encouragement.
He's been abroad several times and is familiar with
foreign ways and customs and, as we've had business
dealings in the past, I've indicated to him that he
should let you have as much money as you need. To
send money by mail is expensive and runs the risk of
getting lost en route; there's no sense in mailing
money. Be sure to get in touch with Chaim
Soroker, give him my regards and tell him I'm
awaiting an answer to the letter I recently wrote
him. Tell him that there's still no news from home.
His Esther hasn't given birth yet. One more thing
I'd like to ask of you, Beltzi dear—keep some
distance from your cousin, Chava'le Tchopnik. Not
because she doesn't have a good reputation on the
Nalevkis—I laugh at those things—but just because
I don't want tongues to wag about you and fingers to
point at you. As you yourself said, Marienbad has

become a miniature Warsaw. All of the Nalevkis, you said, are there this summer. You see that Broni Loiferman and Leah'tzi Broichshtul and even Madam Yamayichke and her daughters are already in Marienbad. What other proof do you need? You have to avoid them like the plague because they are terrible gossips. Better to break a leg than to fall into Madam Yamayichke's mouth. I will never know why it is so important for Broni Loiferman and Leah'tzi Broichshtul to drag themselves off to Marienbad. Alright, Loiferman, they say, hit it rich this year in the lottery, and the rubles are burning a hole in his pocket. But Broichshtul? Just last week he came to see me about getting an interest-free loan and I told him where to get off. Asking for an interest-free loan and sending your wife to Marienbad—for that you really have to have nerve!

As for your writing that I should look after everything in the house—don't you worry about a thing. You just see to it that you get better and come home safely and then everything will be all right. Your worries about Sheva-Rochel are a waste of time. First of all, she's proven many times over that she's honest, even if there were gold lying around, and second of all, I really am keeping a close eye on everything; not only the sugar canister but the bread is under lock and key. I too am reluctant to buy on credit at the market. True, we deal with honest folks, with virtuous folks, but let's face it, some of them can be real thieves at times. Again I urge you, Beltzi dear, not to begrudge yourself anything. You should enjoy yourself there and get the best of everything for yourself. Just one thing I ask—don't go bargain-hunting in the shops. When you come home, I will, God willing, I promise you, buy you anything your heart desires. Why do you need such junk—tablecloths and handkerchiefs—don't you have enough of those already? Why do you need a special machine to make butter? And where will you put a wall clock? I'm just afraid, Beltzi, that when you arrive at the border you'll have such aggravation that all the good that Marienbad did will be thrown out the window and all my money would be wasted. Remember the humiliation Madam Karalnik from the Nalevkis suffered three years ago when she showed up at the border looking a little too plump and was made to go into a separate room where she was stripped down to her undershirt. They unwound from around her body over four hundred yards of silk ribbon. From that time on she was dubbed by all of us on the Nalevkis "the Karalnich'ke with the ribbons."

See to it that you get well soon and return home safely.

Wishing you only the best, I remain,

> Your husband,
> Shlomo Kurlander

5.

*Chaim Soroker from Marienbad to his friend
Shlomo Kurlander on the Nalevkis in
Warsaw.*

Dear friend Shlomo:

I received your heartwarming letter and am so
pleased that you write so openly and consider me as
a true friend. It will please me even more if I can be
of real service to you. That your Beltzi is coming to
Marienbad, I knew even before your letter arrived.
You might want to know in what way and from
whom I found out? Actually from Madam Tchopnik.
How, you say? Let me tell you exactly how it
happened. Since there really is nothing to do here—
one can go crazy from boredom—let me try my hand
at being a writer. I ask only one thing from you,
Shlomo, that everything I write about this place be
strictly confidential. You trusted me to be discreet,
so I too trust you in matters I would not trust
anyone else, not even my own wife. I am positive
these matters will remain between us.

First I must describe Marienbad to you so that you
will know precisely what this place is like. The
people who come here are those whom God has
blessed with an abundance of money and punished

with an abundance of flesh. Perhaps it is really the very opposite—punished with an abundance of money and blessed with an abundance of flesh. These people are the most miserable on earth. They crave food and aren't allowed to eat. They yearn to travel and can't. They desire nothing better than to lie down and aren't permitted. "You must walk, the more the better," say the doctors. "You must lose weight," they say, "the more the better." "Lose weight," translated, means "Lose your ugly, fat belly, slim down." And for fat bellies there is one remedy—Marienbad. Here you lose weight as if it were removed directly by hand. There's nothing surprising about that. For food they give you next to nothing. The doctor forbids you to eat. You survive only because you are permitted to drink a little spring water, or as they call it, *Kreutzbrunen*, in the morning. Drunk warm on an empty stomach, it has the flavor of tepid dishwater. After your drink, you must walk, *exercise*, as the doctor calls it. After such drinking and such exercise you long to bite into something solid. You return to your hotel to eat and they serve you what they call *frishtik*, which turns out not to be food at all. What does this *frishtik* consist of, I ask you? Meat? No. Eggs? No. Rolls? No. A mug of cocoa and a dry zwieback—that's what they call *frishtik*. After *frishtik* the doctor makes you do more *exercise*, and that's when you work up a real appetite. When dinnertime comes around you imagine you could swallow an ox, horns and all. But the doctor says, "No, no, dear man, if you eat like

49

that," says he, "you won't lose so much as an ounce, not an inch of fat, and you won't ever get rid of that excess baggage!"

In a word, it's hell, believe me. Luckily, you can stick your tongue out at the doctor. He orders you to eat nothing—let *him* eat nothing; he insists that you walk—let *him* walk. We're better off sitting down and playing a game of Preference. The problem is that there aren't always the necessary three players, so you have to play Sixty-six with a partner. You know that I really enjoy cardplaying, but there is no one else around with whom to play Sixty-six except for Madam Tchopnik. As unbelievable as you think Berel Tchopnik is, he's nothing compared to his wife. I tell you, there is only one Madam Tchopnik. And she doesn't play half badly either. She can outplay any three men. So why am I complaining, you ask? She hates to lose more than anything in the world. And if she loses, she doesn't pay up. "You know who I am," she says. "You can trust me and, if necessary," says she, "my husband will pay you." What do you say about depending on *him* to pay up? It wouldn't be so bad if playing Sixty-six were the only thing she wanted to do. The problem is she likes to have you stroll with her through Marienbad. Just strolling with her would be tolerable, but the problem is she wants to do more than stroll. To her strolling involves going shopping, bargain-hunting, outwitting a German or two—and before you know it, you are lending her money which you will never see again. What a nuisance, I tell you! You can't

50

hide from her. And just my luck, I'm the only one she seeks out. There's not one other man here from the Nalevkis. Only women. Broni Loiferman, Leah Broichshtul, Madam Sherentzis and Madam Pekelis. There's Madam Yamayichke with her three overgrown mam'selles who are the laughingstock of Marienbad because of their falsified ages. They would be perfectly fine mam'selles if not for their noses. Marienbad this season is full of wives. Everywhere you turn, wives—young wives, old wives, countless wives. Most of them are the ordinary sort from Bialystok, Kishinev, Yekaterinoslav, Kiev, Rostov and Odessa. Wherever they are from, they are here for the so-called "cure." But their main purpose is to corral husbands for their daughters, their ripe mam'selles. These chaperones are dressed in rich silks and satins, they wear pearl necklaces. Their daughters are put on display. The mothers speak pidgin German and inspect every man as if to say, "If you're a bachelor, come here; if you're married, go back to where you came from." Buzzing around these mamas like a bee around honey, is this character with a top hat who is called Svirsky. This Svirsky is a marriage broker, but he calls himself an international matchmaker. He's Jewish but he refuses to speak Yiddish, only German. His word for a successful match is a *partie*, a potential bridegroom is a *bräutigam*; he will never say "your wife," but *eure Frau gemahlen*. I tell you it's quite a sight to see these overstuffed mamas in their pearl necklaces chasing after Herr Svirsky, chattering to him in their bad German while he

51

boasts about his successes, how many *parties* he's arranged, and all based on love. I've met our Madam Yamayichke from the Nalevkis with her three daughters several times strolling about with this Herr Svirsky, who never removes his top hat—not Shabbes, not weekdays. May God help her, I wish with all my heart that Svirsky might arrange a *partie* for her, three *parties*, three *bräutigams* for her three noses even if it's without love, and the sooner the better. You can bet the youngest will have to start lying about her age soon because she's already past thirty. And if we were to add to *her* age the years her older sisters have subtracted, it would altogether, I'm afraid, add up to a total of more than a hundred, poor things! As much as possible, I avoid Madam Yamayichke—you know what a gossip she is.

So now that I've described a little of Marienbad for you, I can tell you how I found out your Beltzi was coming.

Yesterday morning I went to the "watering trough" where I met Madam Tchopnik, Madam Loiferman, Madam Broichshtul, Madam Sherentzis, Madam Pekelis and Madam Yamayichke with all of her three noses, as well as some other women—the whole Marienbad Nalevkis crowd! "Good morning," "Good day," "How is it going?" "What's new?" Meanwhile Chava'le Tchopnik said to me, "Do you know we're expecting a guest in Marienbad tomorrow?" Said I, "God love you and your guest. Who is it?" Said she to me, "Aha, see how clever you are and figure it out." Said I, "What makes you think I can figure it out?" Said she, "I'll give you a clue." Said I, "By all means, let's have a clue," Said she, "Not one clue but several. First of all, she is," said she, "pretty, the prettiest of all the Nalevkis women." That really irked the other women. They exchanged glances and hurled such fiery looks at Madam Tchopnik, you could have burned down a small town in Poland. Madam Tchopnik was oblivious to their reaction and started enumerating the virtues of this pretty newcomer to Marienbad. "Enough of these virtues," said I to her. "Give me another clue." "The other clue," she said, "is that she has a husband who is more than twice her age and she's not even twenty years old."

At this point all the other ladies burst out laughing, "Not counting Saturdays and holidays!" Seeing this could go on all day, I said to Madam Tchopnik, "Enough of this backbiting," said I, "let's hear," said I, "who is coming to Marienbad." Said Madam Tchopnik to me, "Hush! One more clue and that will be all. She is," said she, "a relative of mine." "Is that so?" said I, "so why are you beating around the bush? Just say," said I, "that Beltzi Kurlander is coming to Marienbad and make an end of it." There then ensued a discussion among the women about your Beltzi, and, as usual, talking more than all the others was Madam Yamayichke. What can I tell you, Shlomo? I can't begin to put it down in writing and really don't want to repeat it. You must know yourself what Madam Yamayichke can think up about your Beltzi. And not just about Beltzi, but also about you! If an outsider were to

53

overhear her, he would surely conclude you had ruined her life or done something awful to her.

Fortunately, Herr Svirsky with his top hat joined us and called Madam Yamayichke away to whisper something in her ear, probably about a *partie* or a *bräutigam*.

That's how I found out that your Beltzi was coming to Marienbad. Then when I went home in the evening, I found your letter. You were correct in writing to me. Rest assured, dear friend, that I will do everything you ask of me on your behalf and on hers. You can rely on me. I won't spare any effort and will write you everything as it happens. But you too must not be lazy. Write more often what the news is from Warsaw. But try to write only good news—I hate sad letters. It's a matter of necessity. If I'm here for the cure, I have to forget all about my troubles and misfortunes. There are enough troubles at home the rest of the year. Believe me when I tell you that when I am abroad, I do not even read a newspaper. I do exactly as I please—I eat and drink and sleep and take my stroll and try to lose weight and play a game of Preference if I can find a third hand and if I can't—I play Sixty-six with a partner. So be well. God willing, tomorrow morning, when your Beltzi arrives, I will most likely let you know about everything in greater detail. Again, be well, and continued success in your business. Wishing it so,

> Your best friend,
> Chaim Soroker

6.

Beltzi Kurlander from Marienbad to her husband, Shlomo Kurlander, on the Nalevkis in Warsaw.

To my dear husband, the learned Shlomo may his light shine forever.

This is to let you know I have arrived safely in Marienbad. I was hoping to find Chava'le Tchopnik at the train station. It turns out my cousin hadn't received my last letter from Berlin. That's what she says but I think it's a lie. She received my letter all right, but she didn't have the time to come pick me up at the train. She's so busy playing Sixty-six all day long. Guess with whom. You'll never guess even if you had eighteen heads—with your good friend, Chaim Soroker. Oh, if his Esther only knew! I hate to tell you what I wish on your good friend! He has it good here. They say he's living it up, really skimming the cream off. This I found out from Madam Yamayichke as soon as I arrived. I had the good fortune to run into her and her three little noses at the station waiting room. They were seeing some young man off, supposedly a potential bridegroom they had ensnared, while this clown of a character with a tall chimney on his head was hovering around them. She couldn't talk much with

55

me but nevertheless she managed to tell me loads of news about our Nalevkis crowd in Marienbad, which I will save for another time. But I do want to tell you about my journey from Berlin to Marienbad.

It was an awful journey. And whose fault was it? Yours! Because of your constant complaining about business being bad, I saved money by going third class instead of second class. It was terribly uncomfortable and crowded. There was no room to sit, much less to lie down. The smoke was as thick as in a steam bath. The Germans smoke these smelly cigars that can choke you to death. When you go second class, the customs people treat you very differently than in third class. I can't complain that they found anything in my luggage though. But I can't tell you how terrified I was. I had thought that there was no border between Berlin and Marienbad. They all speak the same language, so why do they need a border? It turns out they do have a border, besides which, the Germans love to poke into things and rummage around. So I was really scared. Especially about the lace more than anything else I had with me. If I had known about the border between Berlin and Marienbad I would have hidden the lace better. I would have sewn it into the heavy quilt like Madam Tchopnik does every year. But I, like a fool, sewed them loosely onto my old dresses which I put into the laundry bag. I thought I would faint when the German customs official asked, *"Vas haben Sie hier?"* I opened the suitcase and said to him, "Old dresses and dirty laundry." He listened carefully and then pointed to the second suitcase, *"Und vas haben Sie hier?"* I opened the second suitcase and up popped your straw hat. I forgot to write that I bought you a straw hat at Wertheimer's in Berlin, a real Panama hat. Can you guess how much it costs? I won't tell you till I get home. You have to guess how much I paid for it. As I was saying, when your Panama hat popped up, I thought I would die. How come I'm carrying a man's hat? I had a bright idea—I know Germans aren't especially smart, so I said to him in German, *"Das ist mein Panama, bei uns in Rusenland tragen alle Damen mansbilishe Panamas."* He didn't answer me, but said, *"Fiehren Sie Russishe tee! Haben Sie zigaretten?"* I thought to myself, "May my troubles be on your head!" and told him I wasn't "carrying" tea and I didn't smoke cigarettes. Then the German took a piece of chalk and made a mark across all my pieces of luggage, packages and baskets, as if to say, "Kosher! Passed inspection!" Who would have guessed that the Germans would have been looking for Russian tea and cigarettes? Wasted fears and wasted worries! But had I gone second class, I would have been spared the worry as well, because in second class, they say, the officials just walk down the aisle asking if anyone has anything to declare. And who is to blame? Only I myself. I'm so terrified of spending an extra groschen of yours. Not that you actually ever say anything, but when it comes time to pay the bills, you have a way of sighing and groaning and letting me know that the money is going. I am just grateful that I was able to find inexpensive lodgings and an honest

57

proprietress in Berlin. You should have seen the small bill Madam Perelzweig handed me when I left Berlin. I thought one of two things—either it was a dream or she was out of her mind. Just imagine—for milk, no charge. Tea and sugar she forgot about. Herring, radishes, onions, chicken liver and more—these she called "snacks." The only charges were for the room and meals—that's all. Tips weren't necessary either, as in other hotels, because she was both servant and owner. I tell you, it wasn't a hotel but paradise. There's good reason why our Nalevkis women stay there. The way she saw me off at the train station! She wouldn't even let me get a porter. Everything herself. And as if that weren't enough, I was given a bouquet of fresh flowers—not from her but from the "arranger," the old bachelor, the imbecile with the red pimples I wrote you about in my previous letter. What an idiot! How quickly he forgot the scolding he got from me on the Friedrichstrasse. Here he was again the next morning pestering me, wanting me to tell him the truth, if what he had heard was so, that I had a husband who was an old man in his eighties. I asked him, "Have you ever been to Odessa?" He answered me "What?" in a Latvian accent (he was a Litvak too on top of all his other troubles). Said I, "In Odessa there's an epidemic of cholera and tuberculosis. Neither of them would be too much for you." Do you think he was at all insulted? As long as God has been making *shlimazels*, He's never created one like this one. He was much worse than the two *shlimazels* God sent my way in my third class

car. But I was at least able to get something from
them. They both gave up their seats for me so that
not only was I able to sit but even lie down for a
nap. But I was afraid—what if they were ruffians?
Who can tell? Actually, they gave the impression of
being very fine men. One introduced himself as a
traveling salesman for three factories in Lodz and
the other one said he owned a lumberyard in
Lomzshe. Two fine *shlimazels!* They refused to call
me "Madam" no matter how much I insisted, but
only "Fraulein" or "Mam'selle." I said, "I beg your
pardon, but I have a husband." They said, "I beg
your pardon, how can you prove it?" So I showed
them my wedding ring and said, "Isn't this enough?"
So one of them, the traveling salesman for three
factories, bent over me, studied my finger and kissed
my hand. So I drew back and gave him a good slap.
That, I tell you, really worked. Nevertheless, don't
you think they helped me toss my luggage out of the
train window in Marienbad? They were even eager
to have my address in Marienbad, so I told them to
rot. "If I get lonesome for you," said I, "I'll let you
know," said I, "by telegram or messenger."

So, as you see, I didn't have a very good journey.
It was a terrible journey filled with unpleasant
encounters, and besides which I didn't sleep all
night. My head still aches, I'm crippled, stiff all
over and am very tired. That is why I'm not going
to write you anything about Marienbad now. After
I've rested up, looked around and gotten my
bearings, I'll write you everything. Meanwhile, be
well, keep an eye on things in the house and don't

leave everything to Sheva-Rochel. Tell her to take up all the carpets, remove all my winter coats and furs, air them all out well and put more mothballs in them. I am sending you my address. Don't forget, I beg you, to send me money immediately!

From your wife,
Beltzi Kurlander

7.

Chaim Soroker from Marienbad to his wife, Esther Soroker, on the Nalevkis in Warsaw.

Dear Esther,

I thank you very much for the fine letters you write me so often. You should know that for me there is no greater celebration than when I receive a letter from you. Mail is the one bit of pleasure in this dismal Marienbad. If not for the mail, one would go mad. There is nothing to do, no one to be with, no one with whom to exchange a word. And Marienbad itself has remained exactly the same as it was a few years ago—the same overweight men with their "excess baggage" who come here to take off a pound or two, the same stout women with their pearl necklaces seeking husbands for their ripe

60

mam'selles and ensnaring sons-in-law for themselves, the same overdressed Germans who consider themselves more pious than anyone in the world only because they wear a hat at mealtimes and don't shave their beards between Passover and Shevuos. The truth is, I hold them in contempt, these half-Jews!

It's just a shame, Esther, that I'm not a writer. I would have enough material to keep me writing for a long time. And more than anything I would write about our Nalevkis women who, the minute they cross the border, become "ladies," forget our Warsaw language and start speaking German, pidgin German. Many of them, those from Odessa, speak only Russian—but what a Russian it is! Their clothes, their dressing up and showing off to one another! Those hats and the jewelry and the lace! You should see what goes on here! They're everywhere. When they go promenading or congregate at the Café Egerlander, people point them out because they are so noisy. They laugh so loudly and screech so disgracefully you would think they were still on the Nalevkis.

In a word, Esther, Marienbad in these last few years has not changed so much as a hair. In my opinion the Jewish Marienbad has even gone downhill since the British King Edward died several years ago. When I was last in Marienbad, I remember what a fuss was made over Edward, who ate gefilte fish in the biggest Jewish restaurant. Not just the owner of the restaurant—a fat, well-fed German with a nose like a cucumber—was honored

to have the English King eat fish at his place, but
every guest here for the cure, every Jew, was proud
that he was dining in the same place as the British
monarch. There were Jews who wrote home
boasting to their wives that they were eating at the
same table, practically from the same platter, as the
English King, the renowned friend of Israel. There's
nothing like that any more in Marienbad. One can
easily say that King Edward's death had a greater
effect on the Marienbad Jews than it did on the rest
of the world.

What else can I write you, dear Esther? I am
enclosing a letter from my friend Shlomo Kurlander.
How do you like the way that blockhead is quaking
in his boots over his Beltzi? And what do you say to
the way he goes on about Berel Tchopnik? When
people say that the Kurlanders are on the dull side,
it is apparently true. What a fool! He thinks I have
nothing better to do here than to look after his
Beltzi. As if there weren't enough Nalevkis wives in
Marienbad, here's still another one. I would think a
Madam Yamayichke with her three daughters would
be enough for Marienbad and suffice for all the
Nalevkis wives. Luckily I'm the kind of man who
keeps his distance not only from the Nalevkis
women but from all the women. I leave them to
your brother-in-law—he's the ladies' man. For him
it's a big deal. But I know you don't like it when I
talk about your Meyer, so I'll shut up—enough of
that. But I do know one thing—if I come here for
the cure, then I must get myself cured, otherwise,
what am I doing here in Marienbad? The boredom

is deadly, the homesickness awful. God willing, the time will pass quickly and I will soon be home. I can only tell you I am doing whatever the doctor prescribes. I follow his instructions to the letter like a devout Jew the Shulchan-Aruch. The doctor is very pleased with my progress. He expects me this time to lose no less and perhaps even more weight than a few years ago. That shouldn't be too hard. It seems to me that I do more exercise here in one day than I do at home in a year. Except for an occasional half-hour nap after a meal, I don't sit down for a minute. And as for cardplaying—don't give it a thought. I haven't laid eyes on a card since I left Warsaw. I eat practically nothing. I keep my diet so strictly that the doctor himself is impressed. He says that all his overweight patients, except for me, suffer from too big an appetite. I am of the belief that if one is here for the cure, one mustn't give in to temptation. We sin enough with our overeating all year at home. Don't you agree? Isn't that so?

You asked me, Esther, what I do all day and how I spend my time. What is there to do in this wasteland of a Marienbad? Either one is at the mineral-water fountain or one is doing exercise or one sits at home reading a book. I have never read so much in my life as I've been reading here in Marienbad. Once in a great while, I take myself to the Café Egerlander for a glass of tea and to read a newspaper. I can't stand the place for very long because of these fat women, these mamas who bring their daughters and then put them on display. I thank God that we have sons, not daughters, and will be spared having to put them on display here when they grow up. Kiss the children, Esther, and be sure to see the doctor once more. Let him tell you exactly when the baby is due. Be well. I kiss you again and again. God willing, you will soon send me a telegram with good news.

Your most devoted husband,
Chaim Soroker

8.

From Madam Yamayiker in Marienbad to her husband, Velvel Yamayiker, on the Nalevkis in Warsaw.

Velvel!

You write that you want me to write you the news, so I'm writing to tell you that so far there's nothing to write about. Nothing, but nothing, has happened. And I'm writing you, Velvel, that I'm afraid nothing will come of this Marienbad. I kept saying we should go to Karlsbad instead of Marienbad because people say everybody goes to Karlsbad. Thousands of the most important marriages are arranged there. But you were stubborn as a mule and insisted on Marienbad. And you, once you've made up your mind, can even three pair of oxen budge you? And I'm writing you, Velvel, still another time, what good is this Marienbad if you don't set eyes on an eligible man to save your life? On the Nalevkis, throw a stick, you hit a dog. In Marienbad, turn around and you run into a mother with a daughter looking for a husband. And since God has blessed me, knock on wood, with three mam'selles, then, it seems to me that I should be somewhere better and not have to put up with this cutthroat competition. And just for spite, this summer there's been a steady stream of mamas with their mam'selles and all are offering these enormous dowries—twenty thousand, thirty thousand, forty thousand! Ten thousand will get you absolutely nowhere. A little doctor from the Liade, who on the Nalevkis would grab ten or fifteen thousand with both hands, here demands a fortune. Even a businessman is worth his weight in gold.

And I'm writing you, Velvel, that till now it hasn't been too pleasant because this Svirsky, the one I wrote you about, the marriage broker, I mean, has brought me three real characters. One of them is a Lodzer from Lodz and appears to be sickly. When he speaks, he speaks with a slight funny gasp, although to look at him, he appears quite nicely dressed, has a fine bearing and says that his father owns a factory in Lodz; it's likely not a factory, but a little business. He will himself receive a dowry, he says, of ten thousand, against which he wants twenty-five thousand. I protested to him, the

65

marriage broker, "For what great achievement does he think he deserves three times as much? Because he has such a nice voice?" So he answered me, this bigtime marriage broker, "First of all, twenty-five thousand," said he, "is only two and a half times as much, not three times as much, and second of all," said he, "you should be thankful that he isn't asking for five times as much. You see for yourself," said he, "what's going on with bridegrooms in Marienbad! Just give me," said he, "three dozen Lodzer young men like him and you'll see," said he, "what I can do with them." So that accounts for one of them. And I'm writing you, Velvel, that the other one is a Bialystoker from Bialystok, also a decent young man and quite well-to-do, but he is already a widower. Actually not a widower, but a divorcé since he's recently, he says, divorced his wife. When I wanted to ask him why he got divorced, the marriage broker wouldn't let me do it. He sat opposite me, the marriage broker, biting his lip and winking at me like a drunken bandit. I told him afterward, the marriage broker, "For God's sake!" said I, "how can I get involved with a person if I don't know," said I, "why he got divorced? What if," said I, "*she* divorced him, not *he her*?" So he answered me, the marriage broker, "First of all, you can tell just by looking at him that *he* divorced *her*, not *she him*, because one simply doesn't divorce such a man. And second of all," said he, "if you start," said he, "picking away at this and at that, you can," said he, "take your business," said he, "back with you to Warsaw on the Nalevkis." So I said to him, "Tell me," said I, "what makes you throw the Warsaw Nalevkis up to me? Don't you think," said I, "we can do just as well there?" "If you can do just as well there," said he, "why did you have to go through the trouble of coming all this distance, and with three daughters into the bargain?" That fox! Back in Warsaw, a man like this Svirsky would go flying down my stairs head over tail, but here he wears a black chimney on his head, yellow gloves on his hands, and calls himself an international matchmaker and people fight over him. And I'm writing you, Velvel, that you can't get anywhere with him because this marriage broker thinks he's an aristocrat. He claims that his matches aren't just arranged like those of ordinary matchmakers but develop out of acquaintanceship and love. First the couple meet, supposedly by accident, but actually it's arranged by the marriage broker. After this they meet at the fountain where you drink spring water, but now without the help of the marriage broker. Then they go to the theater or to a concert—no marriage broker anywhere in sight. And there, at the theater or at the concert, they fall in love, and after they fall in love, they become engaged, and finally, at the engagement, the marriage broker appears and collects his commission. But, God in heaven, how long can one wait? So, I've told you about two bridegrooms. And I'm writing, Velvel, that the third one is a Kishinever from Kishinev, but we really haven't had a chance to look him over carefully because we met him at night. He and the girls happened to meet at the theater. So, I'll write you about him another time. And I'm writing you, Velvel, you can say what you will, we just have no luck when it comes to matches. Take this Lodzer from Lodz who out of the clear blue sky suddenly decides to leave Marienbad. His father, he said, had summoned him back to Lodz. That's what the marriage broker said but it turns out it was a lie. He actually had to go to a sanitarium. And I'm writing you, Velvel, how I found out he was going to a sanitarium and not to Lodz. We had all gone down to the train station, I and the girls and the marriage broker, to see him off. We wanted to make sure the marriage broker wasn't taking him somewhere to look over another bride. Who would put anything past a marriage broker? And I'm writing to you, Velvel, that I listened in very carefully when the marriage broker bought him his ticket, and I heard him say to the cashier, "Badenveiler." I heard this distinctly; I am not deaf. So I said to the marriage broker, "You told me," said I, "he was going to Lodz, but you ended up buying him a ticket to Badenveiler." And he said to me, "What are you talking about? What Badenveiler?" I said to him, "I very clearly heard you say 'Badenveiler,'" said I, "I am not deaf." So he said to me, the marriage broker, "What a strange woman you are! Don't you know," said he, "that Badenveiler is on the other side of Lodz?" And I said to him, "Your nose should only be on the other side of your face," said I, "like Badenveiler is on the other side of Lodz. I think," said I, "that you're sending him to Badenveiler to look over another

68

bride," said I. "Admit it," said I. "Why do you have
to be so underhanded?" The marriage broker then
softened and took me aside. He swore such vows on
the truthfulness of what he was going to tell me that
you would have believed the devil himself. It's true
the young man wasn't in the best of health, not that
he was really sick, but a little feverish. The doctor
had sent him to Badenveiler for a short rest at a
sanitarium. And I'm writing you, Velvel, that I
didn't rest until I had checked out the truth for
myself about this sanitarium in Badenveiler. It turns
out there *is* such a place. So where does that leave
us? For all that, we're still one bridegroom short in
Marienbad. And I'm writing you, Velvel, that this
morning at the train station I met our Shlomo
Kurlander's wife, Beltzi, all dressed up like a bride at
the wedding eve dinner. Meeting her at the station
was our own Mariomchik's son from Odessa, Meyer,
that fake. I saw with my own eyes, I am not blind,
how he helped her into a carriage. And I saw with
my own eyes, I am not blind, how they both went
off together in the same carriage toward town—so
may I see all my children conducted to the wedding
canopy soon, Amen! And I'm writing you, Velvel,
that for the time being, I haven't anything to write
you about the second bridegroom, the Bialystoker
from Bialystok, because I'm not too pleased with the
fact that he is rather friendly with Madam
Tchopnik. How does he come to Madam Tchopnik?
Well, if our Chaim Soroker from the Nalevkis is the
best of friends with her, it's because he plays Sixty-
six with her day and night. Pity his poor wife,

Esther. But what's going on between this Bialystoker young man from Bialystok and Madam Tchopnik? And I'm writing you, Velvel, that I'm still looking over this Bialystoker from Bialystok very carefully. Whatever I find out, I will write you. Meanwhile, write me why you don't write and what's going on at home. Be well. Your children greet you warmly. Send the other children my love.

From me, your faithful wife,
Pearl Yamayiker

9.

Shlomo Kurlander on the Nalevkis in Warsaw to his wife, Beltzi Kurlander, in Marienbad.

To my dear wife, Beltzi, long may she live.

Your letter telling me of your safe arrival in Marienbad was most welcome. Thank God you escaped from that accursed Berlin with its Wertheimers, those money doctors and those foolish old bachelors, and that you have crossed the border without trouble and arrived safely in Marienbad. It's unbelievable what happened to you. Many Jews go to Marienbad and none run into the problems you did. First of all, why did you have to go third class?

You put the blame entirely on me. I don't
understand how you can believe that when I have
told you a thousand times not to scrimp on yourself.
When I *do* complain occasionally that too much is
being spent, what I have in mind is money being
thrown out, squandered on nonsense. But when it's
a matter of health, money means absolutely nothing
to me. The proof of it is, before you left, while still
at the Warsaw train station, I practically had to
force you to take an extra hundred, almost begging
you to take it. So how can you accuse me of
begrudging you, God forbid, an extra groschen or of
keeping close watch on your expenses? You know
very well, Beltzi dear, how important your health is
to me. No matter if the tenants pay their rent, no
matter if the building business is good or bad, just as
long as you need anything—there will always be
enough, and, God willing, that will always be the
case. And I also must tell you, Beltzi dear, that I
don't distrust you in the least, God forbid. I have
trusted you totally from the first minute we met and
I know that these Casanovas are everywhere, both
here (remember a year ago in Falenitza?) and also in
Berlin and on the train to Marienbad, but they
mean as much to me as last year's snow. I know
how you despise them because you are a pure,
virtuous soul who is devoted to her husband to
whom you have entrusted yourself because you know
he is devoted to you body and soul. Therefore there
is nothing you can do that would make me think,
God forbid, badly of you. Believe me, I know very
well that the flirt who had the audacity to kiss a

strange woman's hand in no way sullied you, just as you weren't affected by that Falenitza *shlimazel* who confessed to me that he was interested in you. Of course, had I been with you in the train, I would have dealt with the Lodzer salesman for three factories differently; I would have broken his head so he wouldn't know what hit him. He would have realized you don't toy with married people. I'm just surprised that you didn't call the conductor and have him throw the scoundrel out. And why did you let such an insolent person help you toss your bags from the train when you arrived at the station? I ask, how could you allow that good-for-nothing old bachelor from Berlin to bring you flowers at the train station after he had spoken so boldly to you on the Friedrichstrasse? Had it been me, the fool would have had the flowers thrown in his face. Who does he think he is, that gigolo, sending you gifts, bringing you bouquets? We have a saying, "As a person deals with himself, so God deals with him." I don't mean to offend you, heaven forbid, I only mean that every person has to have self-respect and protect his reputation and not permit scandal to touch him. How dare that idiot from Lodz have the gall to kiss your hand, on a train, in front of all those people! Thank God one of our Nalevkis townspeople wasn't sitting nearby, and good for you for not telling them your name. Let those dogs croak rather than know who you are.

But these things don't matter a bit to me. I wanted to write you, Beltzi dear, about something else, but I must insist it remain between us—no one

72

can know of this—it's a secret. I practically had to swear on my life not to write you a word of this; so here's the story.

You wrote that you encountered Madam Yamayichke from the Nalevkis at the Marienbad train station. If only you had not run into her it would have saved me a good deal of embarrassment and I would be feeling a lot better. I met Madam Yamayichke's husband today on Gensha Street and he said to me, "I have regards for you," said he, "from your wife in Marienbad." Said I, "Thanks for the greeting. What were you doing in Marienbad?" Said he, "Not I," said he, "My wife is in Marienbad now for the cure. She's doing very well." "Thank God for that," said I, "What does your wife write from Marienbad?" He then took out a long letter, swore me to secrecy, unfolded it and showed me a few sentences. I thought I would faint from shock! She was writing him, Madam Yamayichke, the following (I am writing you her exact words). "And I'm writing you, Velvel, that this morning at the train station I met," she writes, "our Shlomo Kurlander's second wife, Beltzi, all dressed up," she writes, "like a bride at the wedding eve dinner. Meeting her at the station," she writes, "was our own Mariomchik's son, Meyer, that fake. I saw with my own eyes," she writes, "how they both went off together, Meyer and Beltzi, in the same carriage—so may I see," she writes, "all my children conducted to the wedding canopy." So, how does that strike you? Naturally I told him it was a lie. "Your wife was obviously mistaken. That wasn't Meyer

73

Mariomchik," said I, "but my friend Chaim Soroker, because I wrote to him," said I, "that my Beltzi was arriving that day in Marienbad." That's what I said to Madam Yamayichke's husband and that's what I myself believed. But then I arrived home and reread your letter in which you wrote that you really did encounter Madam Yamayichke at the Marienbad train station and that your cousin, Chava'le Tchopnik, wasn't there to meet you because she was sitting and playing Sixty-six with Chaim Soroker. So it's obvious that it wasn't *Chaim*, and since it wasn't Chaim, who then was it?

I simply cannot believe, Beltzi dear, that it was Meyer Mariomchik because it seems to me you hardly know him. And especially since you yourself wrote that he is a deceiver who is making his wife, Chan'tzi, suffer. Unless you've gotten to know him better recently, perhaps through Chaim Soroker's wife, Esther? It seems to me, if that were the case, you could at least have told me that you've become friendly with the good-for-nothing. But since you didn't tell me, I take this to mean that you aren't too friendly with him. And as you aren't too friendly with him, it couldn't possibly be him. If that is so, the same question arises—just who *was* this young man who picked you up at the train station and how did he know when you were coming? Of course, I know this whole story is an utter falsehood since its source is Madam Yamayichke, so I therefore beg you, Beltzi dear, if it is a lie, don't be angry at me for writing you these things which I have no basis for believing. Once again, I beg you to get in touch with my good friend Chaim Soroker and feel free to borrow money from him, whenever and however much you need, and don't scrimp any money on yourself or your health. Enjoy all there is to be enjoyed and come home, God willing, healthy and strong.

> Wishing it so,
> Your husband, Shlomo
> Kurlander

10.

*Chaim Soroker in Marienbad to his friend
Shlomo Kurlander on the Nalevkis in
Warsaw.*

Dear friend Shlomo,

At last I can write you news of your Beltzi. She is, thank God, here safely in Marienbad. I bumped into her but didn't have the opportunity to speak more than a minute with her for reasons not of my making. But let me describe it exactly as it happened. You know that when I tell a story, I love to tell it in every detail and with all the trimmings.

As I recounted to you in my previous letter, here in Marienbad we are almost always outdoors

promenading. One doesn't so much as lift a finger to
do anything useful. Instead we stroll up and down
the avenues, nodding to this one and to that one,
exchanging greetings and continuing on our way
without any purpose other than to "lose one's
belly."

Anyway, as I was strolling this evening after
dinner "losing my belly," who should I see but my
wife's brother-in-law, Meyer Mariomchik, with a
rather attractive young woman who was wearing an
enormous wide-brimmed hat, the two of them quite
friendly, her arm through his. Well—that my wife's
brother-in-law has a way with attractive young
women I don't have to tell you. Everyone on the
Nalevkis knows him—who *doesn't* know Meyer'l,
the Womanizer? My poor father-in-law had to shell
out enough till he finally landed this bargain for his
youngest daughter. I said at the time to my Esther,
"Listen to me, Esther," said I, "this fellow is not to
my liking. He's too much the dandy," said I, "and
too much of a ladies' man for your Chan'tzi." But
she is, after all, a woman, so she said, "When you
were a bachelor, weren't you a ladies' man too? You
would still be one," said she, "except. . . ." "Except
what?" said I. "Except nothing—forget it. . . ." Her
voice trailed off and she uttered a few more phrases
under her breath the way women often do.

As I was saying, I saw my brother-in-law walking
rather cozily with this beauty and I thought to
myself, God Almighty! Who can this woman be?
Somehow she looks familiar but for the life of me I
can't think who she is. Suddenly a thought ran

through my mind: Wait a minute! Can this be Beltzi? Yesterday was the day your Beltzi was supposed to have arrived from Berlin. But in the first place, what business does she have with Meyer Mariomchik? And in the second place, how come arm in arm? When did they become so friendly? Meanwhile, as I was standing and puzzling all this over, who should show up but Madam Yamayichke with all her three mam'selles.

"Good morning."

"Good day."

"What do you think of that couple?"

"What couple?"

"Your Meyer Mariomchik and Shlomo Kurlander's wife."

Said I, "How does he come to know her?" Said she, "Aha! I saw the two of them yesterday at the railroad station. It appears," said she, "that it was prearranged, otherwise, how," said she, "would your brother-in-law know when Shlomo Kurlander's young wife was arriving?"

And Madam Yamayichke then carried on in her usual exaggerated way. It was my thought, however, that my brother-in-law must have found out about Beltzi's arrival from Madam Tchopnik. Madam Tchopnik spread it all over Marienbad that your Beltzi was coming. She showed everyone the letters Beltzi wrote to her from Berlin. I myself was about to go down to the station to meet Beltzi but I didn't know on which train she was arriving. Also that Tchopnik woman had me so befuddled yesterday with her game of Sixty-six that all night long I kept dreaming about "forties" mixed up with "twenties," and in my sleep I kept on dealing cards. Meanwhile I missed your Beltzi's arrival, but my brother-in-law apparently made sure *not* to miss it and it is most likely true that he did pick her up at the train station. So it appears. But let me continue where I left off talking about Madam Yamayichke.

When I heard from Madam Yamayichke that this *was* Beltzi, I immediately protested that I didn't have time to listen to gossip. "I must," said I, "continue my exercise," and set out after the couple walking quickly and finally catching up with them at the entrance of a hotel. Imagine, she was actually staying at the same hotel as he! That I hadn't counted on. Believe me, Shlomo, it's easy to make too much of such small things. People wind up at the same hotel for all kinds of reasons. Nevertheless, I didn't like the looks of it. It would be far better if she would stay elsewhere.

To continue. I allowed a few minutes to pass till they said their goodbyes and parted. I entered the hotel, walked up to your Beltzi, acting as if I knew nothing, just as if you hadn't written a thing to me about her coming to Marienbad.

"Look who's here! Welcome!" said I. "How are you? How is your Shlomo? What are you doing here in Marienbad?" Said she, "The same as you." Said I, "You're here for the cure?" Said she, "What else?" Said I, "With such healthy looks?" Said she, "You can't tell from appearances that a person's shoe is pinching." "Would you like me to show you Marienbad?" said I. Said she, "Thanks, I've already

78

seen all of Marienbad." Said I, "Perhaps you'd like something to eat? If you'd like to go to a kosher restaurant, I'd be happy to take you to one." Said she, "Thanks, someone's already taken me to one." Said I, "Who?" Said she, "Meyer Mariomchik." This cut me like a knife blade through the heart. Where does he come to your Beltzi? He should feel privileged, that scoundrel, to receive even so much as a "Good morning" from her, let alone escorting her all over Marienbad and taking her to restaurants. All of this doesn't bother me. I've known your Beltzi a long time, you understand, and I know that your Beltzi knows him for what he is. Who *doesn't* know Meyer'l Womanizer? The question is—what will other people say? Here in Marienbad, you must understand, people come from all over. Most of them are idlers who come here, as I wrote you, to do nothing more than lose weight. They are up to their ears in money and status. They eat and they drink and they sleep and they spruce themselves up and they take their promenades and they notice who is walking with whom, who is sitting with whom and who is laughing with whom. If they see a pretty woman with a nattily dressed young man, they start to wonder, Now who is he? And who is she? They start to make up stories, exaggerations and outright lies just like we do on the Nalevkis. Once you fall into their mouths, you're lost. And you can assume, naturally, the Yamayichke is right there in the middle of it—*nu-nu!* I don't mean to alarm you, God forbid. I only wish that Beltzi would avoid having anything to do

79

with people who can do harm to her, to you and to your marriage. And especially after your letter in which you asked me to keep an eye on her. I said to myself, "Whatever happens, the first thing we must attend to is to arrange for different lodgings for your Beltzi." There are certainly enough hotels and furnished rooms in Marienbad. You needn't worry, you can be sure I will provide her with a place to stay, with a doctor and with everything she needs. And should she want for money, I will be happy to lend her some. As you write me, not all at once, but a little at a time. You can rely on me. I too have a wife and understand perfectly. All women are cut from the same cloth. A woman may be the cleverest in the world, no sooner does she walk past a showcase filled with cheap rags than her good sense evaporates, of course. You needn't write any of this to Beltzi. As I've already written, you must treat my letters as a sacred trust. She doesn't even have to know that we are corresponding about her. Leave it to me, Shlomo, you have in me a staunch guardian who knows his way around this Marienbad and whose name is—

Chaim Soroker

11.

*Velvel Yamayiker on the Nalevkis in Warsaw
to his wife, Pearl Yamayiker, in Marienbad.*

To my worthy wife, Mrs. Pearl Yamayiker,

I am in receipt of your letter. As to your
complaint that Karlsbad would have been better
than Marienbad, recall that I have repeatedly told
you that Karlsbad would not do for various reasons.
Firstly, according to my best understanding,
Karlsbad is a place for invalids, sick people with real
illnesses, above all for those who suffer from
stomach ailments. Now it follows logically that no
bridegroom would be there, for I am certain that
stomach ailments affect old people, not young men.
And furthermore, I have never heard of any
respectable match being negotiated in Karlsbad, as
you suggest. Whoever told you that everybody goes
to Karlsbad is either a liar or a fool. If I chose
Marienbad, it was for good reason and with
forethought. I am not crazy and know whereof I
speak. Although I personally have never been to
Marienbad, according to respected opinion
Marienbad is a place for pleasure and luxurious
living. Those who go there are the kind of people
who do not feel in exactly perfect health or, quite
the opposite, those who are in too good health and

whose main purpose is nothing more than to trim off a few pounds like our friend Chaim Soroker, a person of sizable proportions, or the kind of people who find their satisfactions in simply looking on as others enjoy worldly pleasures. Accordingly, it is far easier to find a decent match there than in the other place.

And that which you write me concerning the young doctors who can be picked up on the Nalevkis for ten thousand rubles, you are, begging your pardon, greatly mistaken. This kind of merchandise is lately in great demand here in Warsaw. The young doctors you describe are now going for no less than twenty or thirty thousand. This follows logically from the fact that as the government quotas imposed on our Jewish young people in the gymnasia and the universities grow smaller, the young doctors and lawyers grow more expensive, and if these quotas continue to dwindle, God knows where it will all end.

And that which you write me concerning making matches with businessmen, I certainly am not in agreement with you that it's become more expensive. In fact, I believe quite the opposite, based on respected opinion and natural law, because there's a plentiful supply of merchants in the Diaspora. Sound judgment leads me to wonder about your haste in pursuing this match with that young Lodzer manufacturer. Young Lodzer manufacturers can be gotten here too. You don't have to go to Marienbad for them. And particularly when that one isn't in perfect health, it certainly isn't worth the bother.

And that which you write me concerning the Bialystoker, I don't comprehend the reason why you're so unsure and hesitant. In any case you will want to know who divorced whom—he, her or she, him. Send me his name and I'll dispatch a letter to my contacts in Bialystok and I'll soon get to the bottom of it. In fact, I'm surprised that you yourself didn't think of this because these facts are available and Warsaw and Bialystok are almost like one city.

Last, but not least, that which you write me concerning the Kishinever from Kishinev—there you are on the right track because I prefer a bridegroom from Bessarabia to one from Latvia. I am myself from Bessarabia and it appeals to me to have a bridegroom from Bessarabia, in particular from Kishinev, which isn't far from my native village of Yamayke. I can write a letter to my Yamayke relatives who can investigate this Kishinever from Kishinev. I beg you to write me his first name and the name of his family and, with God's help, it will work out for the best. It is long overdue. May our merciful Father in heaven have pity on us and may we make good matches for our daughters, and then we can pay attention to the other children. For the time being, our son Yaakov, may he live to a ripe old age, is doing very well in his studies. He is preparing for his examinations with his tutor. May he pass them soon with God's help because he is beginning to look like a ghost. Even if, God willing, he passes his examinations, I still don't know what will become of him. Never mind a *cheder* education, never mind Jewish studies, at least let him come out with some professional certification. Perhaps it will come in handy in the future. Of course, I would wish better for him. Our son Yaakov, may he live to a ripe old age, should really become a businessman like all Jews. But since nowadays it's the style to have diplomas and certificates, let him also get his bit of a degree, at least at the sixth level. Our son Mendel, may he live to a ripe old age, also doesn't want to go to *cheder* anymore to learn God's ways. I talked to his teacher and the teacher said he was going to need at least two years to prepare him for the third level of *cheder*. I don't know what to do, whether to take Mendel out of *cheder* or not.

And that which you write me concerning Shlomo Kurlander's wife—recall how often I've told you that, as everyone should know by now, Shlomo is crazy to have taken a young bride in his old age, and, besides that, he has committed a grievous injustice against the children of his first wife. But I don't want to get involved in other people's affairs. We have more than enough troubles of our own. Business is slow because the current heat wave is unbearable.

And that which you write me concerning Madam Tchopnik and Chaim Soroker, recall how often I've told you that Chaim goes to Marienbad not for the cure but in order to have a good time playing cards because, as everyone should know, he loves a good game of cards more than anything. Berel Tchopnik approached me again for a loan and let me know what he had heard about how the matchmaking is going. He told me he's been contacted from quite a few places about our daughters. He also told me in strictest confidence that he has information about

84

the examinations our son Yaakov will be taking, and if you are to believe what he says, it's almost a certainty that the whole thing will have to cost us money. I put him off by telling him that I need to write to you and would give him an answer in a few days. Meanwhile I got rid of him without having to give him a loan.

Remember what I've written you concerning the Kishinever from Kishinev and, for God's sake, write me as soon as possible where things stand and especially his first and last name. Because of the great heat and because I have little extra time, I must be brief. I wish you peace and long life. I send my best to you and the children and beg you to write more frequently of everything.

From me, your husband,

Zev Volf Bar Mendel
Yamayiker

12.

*Beltzi Kurlander from Marienbad to her
husband, Shlomo Kurlander, on the Nalevkis
in Warsaw.*

My dear husband the learned Shlomo, may his light shine forever.

I just received your letter and read it over twice. I

85

didn't know whether to laugh at your foolishness or to cry over my miserable luck. You must be aware, Shlomo, you are, after all, a mature man—that what you write is plainly ridiculous. As for your chiding me about the *shmattes* I bought at Wertheimer's—that's just laughable. To you everything is *shmattes*. I remember that last year when I bought a black fox capelet with a sable collar at auction, you also called it a *shmatte*. Not till all the furriers appraised it and said it was a steal worth three times the price did you give in. I can't wait till I come home when I'm all well and you can take a look at these *shmattes* I bought. You yourself will have to agree they are bargains. You really know how to keep the pot boiling. You always manage to do that. But let me tell you, it's no joking matter when you reproach me for not flinging the bouquet of flowers in the face of that gigolo, as you call him. I don't mean to hurt your feelings but when it comes to these things, you're a bit old-fashioned. You have no idea what the real world is like. When you're abroad, it's the custom to escort a departing visitor to the train station whether he likes it or not, and to present him with flowers—*that* is a must. You might be thinking, "The hell with him," but here's a bouquet anyway. If someone is kind enough and polite enough to present you with a bouquet of flowers, no matter what you think of him, you must accept the bouquet with a smile and must say, "Thank you very much." Yes, Shlomo, that's the way of the world. The old ways don't apply nowadays.

And as for your saying that you would have broken the bones of that *schlimazel* of a traveling salesman I met on the train—I really had a good laugh at that. Tell me, what did he actually *do* to deserve having his bones broken? What was his great crime? Did he bite my fingertips off when he touched his lips to them? I made a point of writing you that he received a good slap from me. What more do you want? But your main complaint boils down to one thing—why I rode with Meyer Mariomchik for less than fifteen minutes from the Marienbad train station into town. God Almighty! What isn't going on in Marienbad! What would you say if you were to see our own pious women from Nalevkis, Madam Sherentzis and Madam Pekelis, strolling about, boldly and brazenly, with utter strangers, young men, and at night too? Or, for instance, what would you say if you were to hear what my cousin, Chava'le Tchopnik, describes about the spa at Ostend—she was in Ostend—how men and women swim together nowadays without even so much as a wooden partition between them for appearances' sake, as we have, but to say it plain and simple, they splash together, swim together in the same ocean and even hold hands? She says they only wear these bathing costumes—short, flesh-colored pants designed especially, she tells me, for ocean bathing.

It's another world today, Shlomo, a world that is open-minded and liberal. You yourself have told me many times that wearing a wig doesn't make a woman pious, and keeping her own hair doesn't make a loose woman—so what makes you write such nonsense?

You pose a question: What brought this womanizer, Mariomchik, to the Marienbad train station and how did he know I would be arriving? Now that's really a clever question! I see you don't know anything about Marienbad. You think Marienbad is just Marienbad? Marienbad is Berdichev, Marienbad is Warsaw, Marienbad is the Nalevkis. Everyone knows what's cooking in the other person's pot. You should hear what Madam Yamayichke has to say about Broni Loiferman, about Leah'tzi Broichshtul, about Madam Sherentzis and Madam Pekelis! Or, you should hear what they all have to say about Madam Yamayichke with her three daughters and their matches and bridegrooms—your hair would stand on end! Just let someone drop a word at the fountain, or in a café, or in the restaurant, and in no time it has spread all over Marienbad. I'll give you an example. When I was in Berlin, I wrote to my cousin Chava'le Tchopnik that I was coming to Marienbad. The very next day all of Marienbad, from one end to the next, knew I was arriving, on which train, at what time and even what kind of hat I would be wearing. He thinks he knows Marienbad! And since my cousin was, as I've already written you, so busy with your dear friend Chaim Soroker (they were playing Sixty-six), and since Meyer Mariomchik happened that day to be at the station, mailing, he said, an important letter to Odessa, he noticed a familiar-looking woman (me actually) standing surrounded

by packages and luggage, all alone on the platform.
So he came over and said to me in his Odessa
dialect, half Russian, half Yiddish, "If I'm not
mistaken," said he, "aren't you an acquaintance
from the Warsaw Nalevkis?" So I answered him in
his dialect, "It's possible you aren't mistaken." His
face lit up and he continued, "If I'm not mistaken,
haven't I met you at Madam Soroker's on the
Nalevkis?" So I said to him again, "It's entirely
possible you aren't mistaken." He didn't lose a
moment and said, "Then if I'm not mistaken, you
must be the second wife of Herr Kurlander." I
became a little irritated and snapped, "What do I
care if you're mistaken or not? You ought to take a
closer look at how I'm standing out here on the
platform with all this luggage without a porter,
without a cab, without any help at all!" No sooner
did I utter these words than my companion sprang
into action, brought over a porter, hired a cab,
seated me in it and then sat down alongside me as
we drove into town. Should I have said to him,
"Look here, you'd better get out and walk"? One
more thing—I thought that Madam Yamayichke,
who was, as I wrote you, on the platform, didn't see
us—may she go blind!

But let's assume that all of Marienbad, that is, all
of the Warsaw Nalevkis *did* see us drive off
together—so what of it? How would it have been
different, I ask you, if your friend Chaim Soroker
had been at the station, as you would have
preferred, instead of Mariomchik, and I would have
driven into town with him? Would that have been

easier for you to accept? Isn't Chaim Soroker from Warsaw and isn't he married too? Why did you have to cause me so much needless aggravation with your indignation that I sat down and cried for three hours on end? For *this* I had to come to Marienbad to spend so much money and to ruin what little health I had left on account of your foolish thoughts and fantasies?

No, Shlomo, your letter deserves to be laughed at, not cried over, just as I laughed a few years ago in Falenitza when you flew off the handle at that manufacturer just for saying that he thought I was the prettiest woman from Warsaw in Falenitza. You were fully prepared, if you remember, to tear him limb from limb. And why? What had he done? Weren't you yourself worried afterward that you had made a fool of yourself?

And in this letter of yours, don't you write that you aren't at all concerned with what others think? That's how it always is with you—first you speak, then you're sorry. You yourself write me not to worry about a thing, that you have, God forbid, no suspicions about me and so on. Then you make all these accusations, causing me so much heartache that I have no energy left to take care of myself here. You have the nerve to urge me to get well and come home healthy. How can I get well when I receive such letters from you? What difference does it make what I eat and what I drink and what I buy for myself if you count every groschen and call everything I buy *shmattes*?

I am so upset and nervous because of your letter,

Shlomo, that I can hardly write another line. The Berlin specialists emphatically advised me a hundred times, if they told me once, not to get upset. I should eat, they said, and drink and go for walks and be calm. In Marienbad, you have to be, they said, calm, not nervous, or else, they said, Marienbad and the whole cure are wasted.

There's no more news to write. Tomorrow or the day after I will likely write more. Meanwhile, be well and tell Sheva-Rochel not to forget that summertime isn't wintertime. Summertime you have to beat the upholstered furniture daily and shut the windows to keep the dust and flies out. Also the shutters, to keep the strong rays of sun from fading the curtains. I plan on returning home via Berlin when I'm all better and then I'll buy her a gift of a jacket or else I'll give her one of my old jackets. Don't be such an old woman and write a happy letter once in a while.

From me, your wife,
Beltzi Kurlander

13.

Meyer Mariomchik from Marienbad to his wife, Chan'tzi Mariomchik, on the Nalevkis.

For no reason, *dushinka,* you accuse me of writing you only once every two weeks. To me it seems that I am writing you every day. What else is there to do here in this Marienbad where the heat is oppressive and you don't see a living soul other than our high-flown Warsaw ladies? I avoid them like the plague because you know my attitude toward women in general and how I especially dislike these Nalevkis gossips. We in Odessa dislike gossips. In our Odessa you can walk on your hands and whose business is it? For instance, does it bother me that your brother-in-law Chaim is attentive to Shlomo Kurlander's pretty wife? And in what way is he attentive? He lends her money on Shlomo's account. He says that Shlomo Kurlander personally requested that he should give her money. But whose business is it? Or, for instance, do I care that he plays, your brother-in-law, Sixty-six with Madam Tchopnik every day? Tell me, what would you say, *dushinka,* if you would see me playing Sixty-six with a strange woman? But whose business is it? Or, for instance, is it my business that Mmes Sherentzis and Pekelis,. those two pious young women who, on the Nalevkis, wouldn't dare say a word out loud to a

man, here have cast off their wigs and stroll arm in
arm with this Kishinever gigolo, a flirt who is
chasing after all three Yamayichke's daughters while
Yamayichke herself is chasing after him, just dying
to make a match, though there's a greater likelihood
that I will become a rabbi before that happens
because the Kishinever fop is, at the same time,
carrying on a love affair with Beltzi Kurlander and is
quite serious about it? I have a feeling he's already
propositioned her and she turned him down flat. In
the first place, I know this from a reliable source,
actually from Yamayichke herself. She is, after all, a
close relative of mine. In the second place, I heard
from a close friend, the international matchmaker,
Svirsky, that they are setting up many other
matches for that fop and whatever match they
arrange he agrees to. So they sent inquiries about
him to several people in Kishinev and are awaiting
references. But whose business is it? Only one thing
is important to me—I have to get well and come
home, the sooner the better, to my Chan'tzi, who is
dearer to me than anyone. I beg you, *lyubenyu*, not
to pay attention to what the Nalevkis gossips tell
you and to stop being suspicious because that has a
bad effect on your nerves and you become
unnecessarily anxious. That affects your health and
it doesn't help me feel better either.

What you write me, *dushinka*, about the
business—I advise you that you had better face the
fact that you must make a settlement. My Papa says
the same. You can say what you will, I've said it
before and I say it again, I don't approve of your

brother-in-law's deals because your brother-in-law is a cheat. My Papa says the same. It would be far better for all of us if he were to pay you your share and let *him* remain in the business. That's my opinion and my Papa's too, but you do as you see fit. Whose business is it?

So be well, *lyubenyu*. I want to buy you something I saw here in Marienbad, a kimono. It's all the rage here with wide, short sleeves and with a hood in the back. I don't know which color you like best—black and red plaid or perhaps a pastel shade. I've met very few of our Odessa acquaintances and these are mostly women, as their husbands are in Basel at the Zionist Congress. And since I dislike having anything to do with women, because women at these health spas are mostly gossips, I go around all by myself and am so bored that I'm counting the days when the season is over and I will be able to come home to my *dushinka* Chan'tzi. And since I have nothing to do, I've written a poem about my cousin Yamayichke's daughters, who are picky and choosy but can't seem to pick or choose any bridegrooms. I call this poem "The Proud Bride," and this is how it goes:

Once upon a time in famous Warsaw town
There lived a girl—refined, respected, of maidenly
    renown.
Erect at the piano
She sang French through her nose,
Read every new novel,

Could strike any pose.
Her summers were spent in broadening travel,
That she had but one flaw made her more of a
    marvel.
Money was lacking, you are supposing, I'm sure,
As too often happens to those who are poor.
But your estimate's off by much more than a penny,
Money was plentiful, suitors were many.
I need only tell you this one thing about her—
The bride was too proud, too much was allowed her.
She was spoiled, as they say—rotten.
Too demanding, capricious, her way too much
    gotten.
"As Reb Velvel's daughter I must think of my
    position.
I deserve nothing less than a wealthy physician;
Not an ordinary dentist,
Or druggist, or any *schlimazel*,
Not a learned doctor turned Zionist
Who runs off to Basel.
Never! A doctor of medicine, young, tall and dark
With an office on the Nalevkis overlooking the
    park.
On social occasions he'd shine with style,
His name would be Paul or Jacques or Lyle."
In a word, a serious search got under way,
Continuing for many and many a day.
Matchmakers worked overtime, exhausting their
    files,
Sent telegrams, made trips, no matter the miles.
But a doctor of medicine, young, tall and dark

With an office on the Nalevkis overlooking the
    park,
Whose name would be Paul or Jacques or Lyle,
They—would you believe it?—could not find,
Not if you died for it, or went out of your mind.
This one's too young, that one's not nice,
This one's too tall, that one lacks spice,
And even the one and only
Has his unacceptable list:
Not enough money,
Or he's a Zionist.
In the meantime the years fly by.
As girls grow older,
Suits grow colder.
Only wine improves with long storage
While a woman turns bitter with more age.
In but a few years her troubles are far from few.
She loses—no matter how coddled or sheltered from
    harm—
Her beauty, her freshness, her youthful charm
And she is as useful and valued as an old torn shoe.

So how do you like my poem? Everyone in
Marienbad is reading it. Many have learned it by
heart. And what Yamayichke herself thinks about it,
you will soon find out yourself, as I have learned,
from a letter she is writing you. You should know
that whatever she says about me is utterly baseless.
Also, if by chance you should be on Chlada
Avenue, do step into the newspaper office and give
them this poem and let them look it over, but on
one condition—my name mustn't be printed. It

doesn't help my reputation because it's written in
Yiddish.

Yours, with love and kisses,
Mark Davidovitch Mariomchik

14.

Chava'le Tchopnik from Marienbad to her
husband, Berel Tchopnik, in Warsaw.

Dear Bernard,

You must forgive me for always writing for money
and still more money. I have been up to my ears in
debt. Now at last I've paid most of my bills. Thank
you very much for taking the trouble to wire me the
money I needed. If you hadn't, I don't know what I
would have done. Marienbad is a wasteland;
countless Warsaw women, most of them from the
Nalevkis, and not one with whom you can carry on
a decent conversation. What women! One exactly
like the other. The way they carry on, the way they
dress, the way they live! You should hear the way
they speak. I tell you, you could write a book about
it. Did I say one book? Ten books! Where are all

the writers hiding who write those great articles in the gazettes? Why don't they come here, to the spas, for just one summer—to Marienbad, Karlsbad, Wiesbaden, Ems, Krantz or Ostend? They would have enough material to last them for three winters!

For instance, take my cousin, Beltzi Kurlander. She is, to all appearances, a well-to-do person and doted upon by her husband, that Kurlander blockhead. You'd think she should be able to stay in Marienbad in style—to live and eat in style. You should see the tiny hotel room she's rented—a chicken coop right under the eaves. During the day the sun beats down on the roof and at night you can pass out from the heat. But it's cheap. Nevertheless, when she appears at the fountain in the morning, she is so beautifully dressed and adorned with so much jewelry that the Germans think she must certainly be a princess or a chanteuse. You should see her eating in a kosher restaurant. From the quarter of a chicken she orders, she asks them to save her a piece for later. I am so ashamed for the waiter. The other day she asked for a drink of water and they opened a bottle of Nisshilber for her. When the bill arrived and she realized she was being charged for the water, she became furious! Luckily I was sitting at the same table, so I explained to her in Polish that she should pay quietly and avoid a scene. However often we've sat at the Café Egerlander, I have yet to see her pay for the tea. Either Chaim Soroker pays or our Odesser, Meyer'l Mariomchik. These two fawn over her and she takes full advantage of it, turning on the charm enough to make one sick. There's also a third who helps foot the bill—some kind of Kishinever dentist who is being matched up with one of Yamayichke's daughters. Yamayichke is here in Marienbad with all three daughters and is searching for husbands with a lantern, chasing them through the streets and tugging them by the coattails. But this Kishinever dandy is no fool. A dowry is what he wants from Yamayichke, but the smiles he prefers from Beltzi. But Yamayichke stands guard. Yamayichke is not the kind of woman you can put anything over on. She has eyes that see a long way and a nose that sniffs things out a mile away. She knows exactly from the very first moment which young man is a potential bridegroom and which one isn't. I wanted to suggest a match for her eldest daughter with this jeweler, a very rich man who was throwing his money around. Immediately she said to me, "My pet," she said, "to me he's not a bridegroom," she said. "His fiancée," she said, "is in Kiev, you will soon find out, as sure as you and I are standing here." And it turned out to be so. The matchmaker, Svirsky, was already boasting to me how he had that very morning brought together two cities, Moscow and Kiev, and was thereby earning a fine sum of money. This Svirsky is making heaps of gold. Don't be angry at me, my dear, when I tell you that I've become a matchmaker for a while. I know that things are not easy for you. You really have to rack your brain until you find the money to send me, so I wanted to be of some help to you. At the same time I wanted to do a favor for Yamayichke. Why not?

That one is desperate, dying for a match! And it would be doing a good deed too. It's high time. Yamayichke, if you ask me, is far more respectable than her cousin, the Odesser Womanizer, Meyer'l Mariomchik, and even more so than my own cousin, that rich one, Beltzi. I showed Beltzi your letter in which you wrote me that after Shabbes you would be sending me money. She turned red, then pale, and swore that she didn't have ten crowns to her name. But I know—Chaim Soroker himself told me—that only yesterday he gave her on her husband's account five hundred crowns plus some. Oh! I am sick and tired of such people! Broni Loiferman, as soon as she catches sight of me, starts right in complaining about her husband because he doesn't send her any money. I finally said to her, "Who asked you for this information and why are you telling me all this?" She replied that she wanted people to know what her husband was really like. As everyone knew, he had just won the lottery. Why couldn't he send her a little money on time? I know and everyone knows that's a big lie. Her best friend, Leah'tzi Broichshtul, told me in the strictest of confidence that she herself saw a full purse of money, she swears, in Broni's possession. Naturally she feels she has to tell me, or else I wouldn't know! I ask you, wasn't it much more honest when Yamayichke told me openly and frankly, without any tricks and without any nonsense? "My pet," she said to me, "may you live long," she said, "but from me you won't borrow any money because I won't lend you any. You yourself know," she said, "that your husband, may he be well, owes my husband plenty. If you want," said she, "to earn a nice few hundred crowns, help me out with the Kishinever match." So I'm helping her out as much as I can. I keep telling him, the Kishinever dentist, that it's high time he declared himself to one of Yamayichke's daughters and made an end to it. But he says, "There's plenty of time. Let them get a little older." Is he crazy? We all know that Yamayichke's daughters aren't lacking for years.

Meanwhile this Kishinever puppy is frisking around Beltzi and thinks he has found something really good. I let him know that he was wasting his time because this pretty thing, I told him, with all her charms and coquetry, is a woman who lights the candles every Friday evening and wears an Orthodox wig on her head. But he's so enamored of her that he won't be discouraged. I don't know what she has, that Beltzi. Every man who sees her is her conquest and more than anyone, it seems, Chaim Soroker and the Odesser, Mariomchik. Well, Mariomchik was a womanizer when he lived in Odessa. But Chaim Soroker is a respected businessman and has grown children. Don't think I didn't say to him, "Aren't you ashamed, a man like yourself, an observant Jew, a father, running after pretty women just like your brother-in-law, the Odesser Womanizer? Why do you think he calls himself an Odesser and refers to himself as Mark Davidovitch?"

Quite a reputation this Mark Davidovitch has here. He could bring ruin on himself and it would serve him right if his Chan'tzi would find out about it. I would love to see the day when that Odesser gets his comeuppance if only because he blackens your name to everyone. He swears that his Chan'tzi wrote him that she saw a certain letter written to Esther Soroker by Chaim Soroker from Marienbad. This letter was written by Shlomo Kurlander from Warsaw to Chaim Soroker in Marienbad, and Chaim enclosed it in a letter to his wife, Esther. In it were terrible stories about you and me, Bernard. He even wrote about my birthday dinner party and how you didn't pay Hekselman for the catering and how you lived in Shlomo's apartment without paying him rent for a whole year and how you have lived in Warsaw for twenty years and no one really knows who you are or what you are or what business you're in. There were other such nice things he wrote about you. Mark Davidovitch isn't lazy about showing everyone Chan'tzi's letter. As long as this Odesser flirt is going around wagging his tongue about us, it would be sweet revenge if you would tell some tales on him to his Chan'tzi and keep him so worried about himself that he will forget about us. And I want you to make it good. I'm enclosing a couple of his love letters which he wrote in Marienbad to two Nalevkis wives—Madams Sherentzis and Pekelis—actually good souls. On the Nalevkis they go to *shul* every Shabbes and in the afternoon to the Saxon Gardens—not alone, but with their husbands, those two simpletons. But their husbands, the two Itche-Meyers, must remain outside the garden gates because they are not allowed in wearing their religious garb. You should

102

see how these two pious women have cast off their wigs and long to enjoy the pleasures of Marienbad but don't know how. They've confided in me as in their own sister. You can take their word for it that nothing has happened beyond the letters. I can vouch for them as if it were myself and the letters are the best evidence. But that doesn't really change matters. It's vital that Meyer'l's wife, Chan'tzi, should see these love letters and "enjoy" her husband's adventures. She will immediately recognize his Odesser Yiddish. Let her take careful note of the date on which these notes were written—not as far back as Chmelnitzki's times, God forbid, and not from Odessa but this summer, right here in Marienbad. Just be sure that no one besides Chan'tzi learns about the letters because they were entrusted to me and I gave the two women my word of honor that no one would hear about them. So be well, Bernard. I await good news and remain,

Your beloved wife,
Chava Tchopnik

15.

Meyer Mariomchik from Marienbad to
Madam Sherentzis and Madam Pekelis in
Marienbad.

If I'm not mistaken, we met a year ago in Warsaw
at a Yiddish literary evening on Schweitzarski Place.
As proof: you sat together with your friend and were
bursting with laughter. Mendele Mocher Sforim, the
"Grandfather," from our Odessa, was there and all
Warsaw was honoring him. Another proof: I
approached you and asked you in Russian, "Please,
why are you laughing?" And you answered me, half
in Polish and half in Russian, "Because we are
enjoying ourselves." You exchanged glances with
your friend and ah! I will never forget the sparkle in
your beautiful eyes! Afterward, if you recall, the
three of us walked from the Lazenkis to
Yerushalemski Alley and a bit further. I was
babbling on, recounting anecdotes, and you were
laughing and then you asked my pardon because you
had to leave. So I pardoned you but on one
condition, that we meet again. However, just the
other day, when we met at the fountain, you acted
as if we didn't know one another. I decided that you
must have felt it was improper to speak to a stranger
and that is the reason I am introducing myself with
this letter. You can't imagine what a favorable

impression you have made on me. If I didn't think
my words would sound too forward, I would tell you
that I don't know which of the two of you is the
younger and which one the prettier. It was fated
that our second meeting should take place abroad
and I am very happy because abroad isn't Warsaw
and Marienbad isn't the Nalevkis. I welcome you
and your friend, Madam Pekelis, to Marienbad and I
beg you to accept a bouquet of fresh roses together
with my best wishes.

Your eternal slave,
Mark Davidovitch Mariomchik

16.

*Meyer Mariomchik from Marienbad to
Madam Sherentzis and Madam Pekelis in
Marienbad.*

I am very happy that you feel you understand me;
however, you are mistaken if you take my
sentiments as mere flattery. I assure you that I am a
serious person. All Odessers are like that—there is
no other kind in Odessa. And as for what my
cousin, Madam Yamayichke, and Madam Tchopnik
and the others say—I scoff at that! A spa was meant

for pleasure, not for moralizing. I don't see anything wrong with your becoming friends with an educated person. Tell me, I beg you, why should you suffer more than anyone else in the world? In our Odessa every woman is free and knows no artificial restraints. I am shocked, I tell you, my dears, because in Marienbad it is the other way around. But if you wish to discuss it in greater detail, be at the Café Minion today between three and four. There's too much noise in the Café Egerlander, even worse than in your Warsaw on the Nalevkis. You run into everybody there.

With the greatest impatience I await the two of you.

My regards to Madam Pekelis.

M.D.M.

17.

Meyer Mariomchik from Marienbad to Madam Sherentzis and Madam Pekelis in Marienbad.

You accuse me without cause. I assure you that what I told you today at the fountain is far from flattery. You can take me at my word. In every woman, I appreciate, first of all, intelligence, second

106

of all, tact, and third of all, education. I have
spoken very little to you but believe me, I know you
both as well as if we had been friends for years. And
as to your feeling that I am jealous—Madam Pekelis
hinted at it twice—I swear to you that you are
mistaken. I just said, "What nerve! Look how this
Kishinever boor, this provincial, chases after our
Nalevkis women!" And about my closeness with
Madam Kurlander—that shouldn't surprise you. I
assure you, I am that way with every woman. That's
my way. All Odessers are always gentlemanly and
attentive, although I tell you frankly that Madam
Kurlander is not worth your little pinkies. I know
you both have been burdened with oafish husbands,
those two Itche-Meyers, and have to suffer because
of other people's sins. But Madam Kurlander married
for money and so brought it upon herself. And as to
Madam Pekelis' reminding me that I am a
womanizer, that is, as I see it, beside the point. Do
I deny that I have a wife? I only say that it doesn't
keep me from being friendly with pretty, bright,
educated ladies whenever possible. Accept the
advice of a well-meaning friend and take advantage
of your stay here in Marienbad. By the way, who
told you I write fables, Madam Tchopnik or Madam
Kurlander? And what did they tell you? Where shall
we meet today?

Your M.M.

18.

Meyer Mariomchik from Marienbad to
Madam Sherentzis and Madam Pekelis in
Marienbad.

Our circle in Marienbad has decided unanimously
that your presence is so agreeable that we are taking
the liberty of inviting you together with your friend,
Madam Pekelis, to join us on our outing tomorrow
to Eger. All our intimates will be there and we will
spend the time very pleasantly. We will go rowing
on the lake and I will recite a fable of mine that I
wrote about Yamayichke's daughters. I hope you will
both have a good time. As soon as Madam
Kurlander agrees to join us, you and your friend
must also agree. We are here in Marienbad, not in
Warsaw on the Nalevkis, and must rise above
prejudice.

Your Mark Davidovitch

19.

*Shlomo Kurlander from the Nalevkis in
Warsaw to his wife, Beltzi Kurlander, in
Marienbad.*

To my dear wife Beltzi long may she live.

I received your letter and read it through from
start to finish. I found myself thinking that perhaps
you were right. Perhaps I really am, as you say, old-
fashioned about these things. Perhaps I really am, as
you say, a man of the old school and don't know
what's what. It's possible I'm not that clever
although it seems to me I'm not thought of as a
fool. It's possible you are right that every scoundrel
and every scamp—even an old bachelor with
pimples on his nose who knows how to work all the
angles—no sooner is he in Berlin than he calls
himself a cavalier and can tell strange women that
he has been attracted to them from the moment he
laid eyes on them, and even if you tell him right to
his face that he is a rude idiot, nevertheless, when
the very next day he honors you with a bouquet you
have to feel that this shows his love and you are not
permitted to throw it in his face. It's possible you
are right: Suppose I am riding in a train, who knows
with whom, and I show them a wedding ring and
they start kissing my hand. I'm not allowed to break

109

their bones or throw them out of the train or at least call the conductor and have them thrown out. No! I have to accept favors from them and permit them to help me toss my luggage from the train and then am obliged to accept a thousand compliments from them which make me sick to my stomach. It's possible that I am old-fashioned and can't begin to understand that if there's a young man, an Odesser, who approaches me at the railroad station, a man whom I know to have a reputation as a womanizer, and he stops to ask me who I am and what I am doing here, that I can't say to him, "Who are *you*, sir, and what are *you* doing here?" No, God forbid. On the contrary, I have to make him into a gallant right on the spot and seat myself alongside him in the same carriage and bounce off with him all the way from the station into town so that not only Madam Yamayichke, who all by herself can fill the whole world with gossip, but virtually everyone else, should see how Shlomo Kurlander's wife from the Nalevkis is driving through Marienbad with an Odesser womanizer as bold as you please and is sticking her tongue out at the world. But that's the least of it. If Meyer'l Womanizer is so friendly and takes the trouble to come meet me at the train station and helps me with my luggage and joins me in the same carriage, then I don't dare go where I want to, God forbid, but I must as a social obligation stay at the very same hotel as the Odesser and I must tour Marienbad with him. I must let him take me to a restaurant and sit at the same table so that Yamayichke and Tchopnik and Loiferman and

Broichshtul and Sherentzis and Pekelis—that is, all
Nalevkis from one end to the other—should see
with whom Shlomo Kurlander's wife, Beltzi, is
eating a German dinner. Furthermore, when my
husband's good friend arrives and wishes to convey
regards from my husband, I must dismiss him as
quickly as possible because my husband's friend is,
after all, not a gallant and the other one *is* a gallant
and an Odesser and a gentleman and plainly a
spoiled young upstart who, with his wife's dowry
safely pocketed, does not have to worry about a wife
when there are in Marienbad prettier women, lonely
ones, who, alas, must arrive by themselves in a
strange city and must sit by themselves in a carriage
and go by themselves to a hotel and all by
themselves to a restaurant at noon to eat without
any escort—would that be proper? And suppose that
he *is* a born scoundrel, with whom all of Warsaw
has had trouble—why shouldn't all this bother me?

Why, dear Beltzi, you might ask, am I saying all
these bad things about someone without cause? Here
are some letters from my friend Chaim Soroker. See
what his own brother-in-law has to say about your
fine cavalier and gentleman who has no other name
here on the Nalevkis than Meyer'l Womanizer.

I am certain, Beltzi dear, that when you read over
Soroker's letters, you yourself will see that it would
be far better for you to take my advice and associate
with my good friend, not with Odesser womanizers
who cast their wives off and flit around Marienbad
on the lookout for any attractive young woman who
might be arriving so that they can take her under

111

their wing. And whatever stories Yamayichke will tell you about my friend Chaim Soroker, that he plays Sixty-six with your cousin, Chava'le Tchopnik, day and night, I tell you, Beltzi dear, that first of all, it's a lie, and second of all, even if it *is* true, the one to blame is your cousin, not him. Here's evidence—see what Chaim Soroker has to say about it. They *do* occasionally play a game of Sixty-six because he's bored and there's no one else to play with. But he likes to play with her as much as I like to go dancing, because when she loses, she doesn't pay up. Read over Chaim Soroker's letters carefully and you will see that he covers everything and doesn't leave out even one detail. And when you finish reading the letters, send them back to me because I gave him my word of honor that not a soul would know that he wrote to me.

I think that you yourself will agree with what he writes me because he is a good and true friend and is not "old-fashioned." He is really an intelligent man and a practical one. He understands the ways of the world. So I beg you, Beltzi dear, without fail, as soon as you receive this letter, do get in touch with my friend Chaim Soroker, and whatever you do, don't tell him anything that might lead him to suspect that you know a thing about his letters to me. Just give him my best regards and accept whatever money from him on my account, as much as you need. Don't scrimp on the amount. Another twenty-five or fifty—what's the difference? It's costing enough already! Just remember once and for all, when it comes to your health I do not begrudge you a cent, because in the long run your health is dearer to me than anything in the world.

You should know, Beltzi dear, that your Uncle Moyshe from Rodem visited me and chewed my ear off for a day and a night. He wants me to give him a job in the new house. So I offered him some money but he didn't want any handouts. He wasn't complaining, he said, heaven forbid, or asking for charity, but wanted to earn his bread honestly. I don't know what he meant by "honestly" or what to do with him. And your Uncle Nachman from Kutneh wrote to me and says that everything of his was destroyed in a great fire and he came out of it, he and his family, as naked as the day they were born, and he asks me for help. So I sent him as much as I could, although to tell the truth, the newspapers have not reported any fires in Kutneh. All in all, the money is going up in smoke, and until I get the rent out of these tenants I have to spit blood. The new house has already incurred so much expense that I feel like I'm drowning. But don't give this a thought. I'm not writing you to make excuses so that you will spend less. God forbid! Don't deny yourself anything. Just beware of bad people, of idlers, and of womanizers who don't appreciate their own wives and go looking for prettier ones. You'd do better to depend on my good, true friends. Watch your health, be well and come home healthy, God willing, as I truly wish it.

Your husband,
Shlomo Kurlander

113

20.

*Esther Soroker from the Nalevkis in Warsaw
to her husband, Chaim Soroker, in
Marienbad.*

Dear Chaim,

I am wondering why I haven't heard from you for
so long a time. After that letter in which you
complained about the Marienbad "wasteland,"
where there is nothing to do, you suddenly fell
silent, although I have heard that you write to
others quite often and at great length. It's left for
them to inform me that you have become, with
God's help, a ladies' man in Marienbad, which
boasts, they tell me, very few males and more than
enough females. I would think, Chaim, you must
find it quite agreeable to be, as we used to say, "the
only man in Moscow." True, one has to have a
talent for it and possess a real knack in order to do
justice to so many women, for which I congratulate
you. But I'm not concerned about that. You know,
Chaim, I'm not stupid; jealousy is for other wives,
like my sister Chan'tzi. Pity her miserable luck, she
also hears great news from Marienbad. Good friends
stay up all night and gird themselves in order to
provide her with new surprises about her good-for-
nothing—letters and love notes he sent to all kinds

114

of *dushinkas* and *lyubenyus*. What a reward to have such a brother-in-law like our Mark and what a great thrill and honor it must be to have him for a husband. If you were at home, we would together come up with a solution about what to do with this couple. It's shameful what is happening to my unfortunate sister! Maybe we could help them get a divorce except that Chan'tzi is in love with him, more's the pity, despite all the troubles, and says she can't live without him. Her life is totally ruined! Don't take it amiss, Chaim, that I'm going on like that. How dare I expect you to have in mind these family matters when you have so many responsibilities there? But to return to your letter.

You complain to me, Chaim, that regretfully you are not a writer. If you were a writer, you say, you would have plenty of material to write about from Marienbad. You would set the world on fire. One would think you say this out of modesty. But I must differ with you and compliment you. I never imagined that my husband had such a talent for writing. Your letters are, Chaim, I say without trying to flatter you, perfect examples of the letter-writer's art. Besides the fact that they are so well written, they are also wonderfully varied, each letter with a different tone and with a different subject, even though they were all written at almost the very same time.

For example, the letters you write to your wife are not like the ones you write to your good friends. In the letters you write to your wife, you lament about that Marienbad "wasteland," where you have nothing to do except what the doctors prescribe. You can't eat, you say, you can't rest, you can't so much as touch, God help you, a card. In a word, you are taking the cure, and poor you, suffering so many deprivations, that you are feeling as if exiled to Marienbad. Whereas the letters you write others are much livelier, happier, and read like stories. From the letters you write to others, it's evident that, first of all, you are thumbing your nose at the doctors and actually enjoying a fine appetite, and are spending, thank God, entire days playing three-handed Preference or, in desperation, two-handed Sixty-six. Thank God for Madam Tchopnik, otherwise what would you do if she were not in that Marienbad "wasteland"? With whom would you play Sixty-six? And second of all, it's plain from the letters you write to others how faithfully you've undertaken the care of those poor, unfortunate wives who are going out into the great world all alone for the first time and how seriously you've taken to heart the fact that these lonely wives are strolling about Marienbad without being properly escorted and are dining at restaurants without suitable companions and are staying at the least desirable hotels. I ask you, must you endanger your health, Chaim, packing up and relocating these poor lost souls in nicer hotels and then having to dutifully inform their husbands so that *they* won't miss out on any aggravation and will be worried sick? No, Chaim, to sacrifice yourself altogether for someone else's sake is not worth it. You must not forget that you are there for the cure and shouldn't let yourself get upset, Chaim. Believe me, with God's help, the lonely women will come home in peace to their husbands who were so impatient to remarry immediately after the minimal mourning period and are now trembling in their boots because their wives might, God forbid, go astray. Foolish men! If they would ask me, I would tell them to let these women run loose. Only a cow can be tied down, and even *they* occasionally wander off.

But don't think, Chaim, that the reason I'm writing you in this tone is to convey resentment. You know very well that I'm not like my sister Chan'tzi, who weeps and bemoans her years and days and curses her fate. I just want to call your attention to one thing—the cure in Marienbad can't possibly work if you don't follow the doctors' orders and if you play cards all day and if you eat your heart out on account of strange young women whom you have to watch over so they don't, God help them, get into trouble.

Reading those fine long letters, Chaim, which you write to your "good friends," I was reminded of the good old days which will, alas, never return again. Once, I remember, you also used to write me long, loving, heartfelt letters. Now you write such letters to others and me you get rid of with a few sentences, or else weeks pass and you write nothing at all. But wait, I forgot that you have no time. You have so many responsibilities in that Marienbad "wasteland." May the One above shoulder His responsibilities as well.

Be well, Chaim, and don't forget to drop me a

line once in a while, if only for appearances' sake. Just make believe I'm one of those "good friends" whom you take into your confidence and write to so often and at great length. And I wish you success at Sixty-six and at Preference as in all your other Marienbad affairs.

Esther

21.

Yamayichke from Marienbad to her husband, Velvel Yamayiker, on the Nalevkis in Warsaw.

Velvel! Why are you torturing me, bombarding me with letters, demanding that I write more and more? I *do* write every week, it seems to me, but so far there is nothing to write about because, as you should know very well, we are in Marienbad, not in Karlsbad. And I am writing you, Velvel, that the way the wind is blowing here in Marienbad, even if we were to stay all winter—may our enemies live so long—nothing will happen. And all because of whom? Because of you and your stubbornness and your "considered judgment," which will lead us all, may I be wrong, to a bitter end. Here I thought I had settled things with one suitor, I mean the

Bialystoker, but no sooner do I turn around than off he goes to Basel. Big excitement in Basel! A Zionist Congress has drawn him away to Basel along with other young men who are, as my rotten luck would have it, all Zionists. Luckily, the Kishinever from Kishinev isn't a Zionist; he laughs at the Zionists. He says it's only a pretense, just like those who go for cures. What lies behind them both, he says, is matchmaking. Since that's the case, now I'm really sorry that we came to Marienbad instead of Basel. If I'd known beforehand about a Congress in Basel, I would have gone to Basel because everybody, they say, will be in Basel. And I'm writing you, Velvel, that I already know what you're going to say about that. You will write that I shouldn't write about Basel because according to your "considered judgment" it will come out topsy-turvy, head down and feet up. That's why I don't want to write you anything about Basel because rather than contradict you it's easier to transport Marienbad to the Nalevkis or the Nalevkis to Marienbad. And I'm writing you, Velvel, that you had better get together with those dolts, I mean Hirsch Loiferman, Kalman Broichshtul, Itche-Meyer Sherentzis and Itche-Meyer Pekelis, and especially with Shlomo Kurlander, and ask them who put it into their heads to send their wives off to Marienbad by themselves while they remained at home? They would do better to come here. Let *them* have the satisfaction of seeing how their wives pass the time, how they steal away eligible young men and talk them out of marrying. There's a whole pack of these Nalevkis

119

wives here—supposedly for the cure. What a joke! Day in and day out, all they do is hunt after men—a bachelor, a widower, a divorcé, a married man—anything goes so long as he wears pants. Never in my life have I seen anything like it. When you finally *do* find something with pants, our Nalevkis women land on him like flies. Before you know it, they are sweet-talking him: *hetti-petti-metti-vetti*, in nothing but German, no other language will do. After that they all pair off, presumably to drink coffee but really for more of the *hetti-petti-metti-vetti*, till finally they go off together somewhere on the outskirts of town and there they either go into the woods or go boating—who knows and who cares what they end up doing! And I'm writing you, Velvel, that you write me I should write you about the Kishinever match from Kishinev, so I'm writing you that I've already written you about it. How many times do I have to write you? His name is Zeidener, he's a dentist, and has a nice face. One could say he's a solid person, well-dressed and pleasant to look at, altogether acceptable. And I'm writing you, Velvel, that the matchmaker has already sent off two letters to Kishinev asking them to write him who and what this Zeidener is, and they wrote him that he really is a dentist and a good one, they write, and has a nice office, is very agreeable and makes a fine living. And it's apparent money means nothing to him. He even refuses to talk about money, unlike others, the Bialystoker, for instance, who has been haggling with me for weeks as if over an ox. That is to say, *he's* not doing the

haggling, but the matchmaker is. He himself
pretends to stand off to the side, doesn't get
involved in such matters. And I'm writing you,
Velvel, that I like the Kishinever dentist very much.
I figure that after the wedding I'll have him take our
Yankele under his wing, maybe he can make
something of him. And I'm writing you, Velvel,
that you have no cause to bombard me with letters
telling me to write because so far I don't have
anything to write about. When there is something
to write about, I'll write it to you or send you a wire
telling you to come immediately. And I'm writing
you, Velvel, that I've involved our Madam
Tchopnik in the whole Kishinever matchmaking
affair. She lives the good life here, but money she
never has, so I pushed a little commission her way.
Why should Svirsky, that fancy marriage broker
whom I wrote you about, have the whole pie to
himself? What do I care if Tchopnik bites off a little
piece for herself? Let's just hope it works out well,
God willing, and I will be able to write you good
news. And I'm writing you, Velvel, to find time,
without fail, to get together with Loiferman and
with Broichshtul and especially with the Kurlander
ox. Open his eyes to what his Beltzi is up to. He'd
better start paying attention to his wife rather than
to his houses. His houses won't run away but his
Beltzi is flirting with eligible suitors and other men,
who are fighting over her as if she were a prize. It's
sickening, a crying shame and a heartache at the
same time, because if not for these Nalevkis women,
this Kishinever match would have been safely in our

121

pockets long ago. And I'm writing you, Velvel, that I really can't write you so much. Be well, and give my love to the children, Yankele and Mendel.

From me, your wife,
Pearl Yamayiker

22.

Chaim Soroker from Marienbad to his friend
Shlomo Kurlander on the Nalevkis in
Warsaw.

My friend,

I now see that I have to deal altogether differently with you. It would be far better not to write you at all because you don't deserve it. An imbecile like you, with no brains or integrity, is really beneath consideration! When everybody says that the Kurlanders are blockheads, it's apparently not without cause. The whole world can't be crazy.

I ask you—you're not a jackass, you're a man of almost sixty—give it a little thought, if you can still summon up an ounce of sense, and consider what you've done. You go through the trouble of writing me a letter in which you beg me for a favor. You have a real problem on your hands—your Beltzi is

122

going to Marienbad for the first time in her life, doesn't know the language and is thoroughly befuddled. You want me to befriend her, keep an eye on her, lend her money and other such things. On top of all that I'm supposed to see to it that she keeps her distance from her cousin, Chava'le Tchopnik, and you yourself insist that it remain a secret between us. And I'm fool enough to believe what you've written me and take pity on you, write you first one letter and then another letter telling you everything in the greatest detail, reminding you ten times over that as you wrote me in secret, so also what I am writing you must be considered a holy secret to remain between the two of us, and not another soul must know that you are writing me and I am writing you. So what does a genius like you do? Kurlander turkey that you are, you go straight to my Esther and give her my letters. Don't you deserve to be flogged and flayed in public right in the middle of the Nalevkis? I ask you, lunatic, what person in his right mind does a thing like that? Not even the meanest scoundrel in the world does a thing like that! Not for nothing do people say "A fool is a thousand times worse than a scoundrel." No, let me put to you another question: What possessed you to saddle me with your Beltzi? And what do I care whether your Beltzi is going to Marienbad for the first time or for the last time? Who missed her here in Marienbad, and who was looking for her, except my little brother-in-law, the Womanizer? You should know, you Kurlander dunce, that your Beltzi is not, God forbid, lonely here. In addition to my little brother-in-law, the Odesser playboy, there are plenty of other Casanovas dancing about her. Leading all the rest is this Kishinever dandy with white trousers, a dentist who was about to become engaged. Madam Tchopnik was the big matchmaker and was supposed to get a big commission, but it fizzled out, no one knows why—they're keeping it a secret. Only your Beltzi knows the secret because no one is as close to him as your Beltzi. They are always strolling about together, drinking the waters at the same time from the fountain, and eating at the same table at the restaurant. That really must have gotten to my little brother-in-law, the Odesser, so he started up with the Kishinever dentist and the dentist has challenged him to a duel. Marienbad is in a state of uproar! In a word, it's like a novel and your Beltzi is the heroine. And you continue to sit on the Nalevkis watching your houses. Watch, watch, Kurlander simpleton, so they won't run away! Don't worry about your Beltzi. She won't get lost. I heard say that she was going to leave here for another spa—where, I don't know. I heard it was Ostend. And she's doing the right thing—change of place, change of luck. In any case, you needn't lose any sleep over it. She's not going alone. She's going with an escort, but what do I care? As far as I am concerned, she can go with two escorts, because if you could be so indecent as to show my Esther the letters I wrote you in such great confidence, then you are a louse and a rat and a filthy swine who

124

should be wiped off the face of the earth, and I will have nothing more to do with you!

As a matter of fact, I could now write you lots of news about Beltzi and this Kishinever fly-by-night but I don't want to get involved in your affairs any further. Enough. I've been burnt once by you; let someone else have a turn. Don't ever ask me to do anything for you again and don't write to me because I won't answer you. I am no longer your adviser and your confidant so don't pester me and don't annoy me anymore. I want it to be as if I had never known you.

The money I gave your Beltzi on your account you can send me here, if you wish, and if not, you can pay me in Warsaw in installments. Don't worry, I trust you. But, if you decide not to pay for your Beltzi, well, you'd better not even think of it. I have your letter in which you explicitly ask me to give your wife money on your account whenever she needs it and as much as she needs. If you deny it, you will suffer shame and humiliation because I will have your letter translated into Russian and it will serve as evidence.

And hear me out, genius, since you are, I see, a person who cannot keep a secret. You will certainly show my wife what I'm writing you now, so I'm telling you that you are welcome to do so. But before I end my relationship with you, I must again tell you openly that you are a Kurlander halfwit and a damned fool and a nincompoop and an ox and a jackass, and more that I can't bring myself to say.

From me, your former good friend, whose shoelaces are worth more than you.

Chaim Soroker

23.

Shlomo Kurlander from the Nalevkis in Warsaw to his friend Chaim Soroker in Marienbad.

To my dear respected good friend the learned Chaim may his light shine forever.

Like oil on fire and salt on a wound, that's what your letter was to me. As if I don't have enough problems already, you had to add to my woes and heartache. I am absolutely beside myself and am at a loss to know what to do. It's not enough that I have to hear such good news from Marienbad, I also have to suffer humiliation at your Esther's hands and have to hide my face in shame from Berel Tchopnik whom I avoid like the plague. If I were to bare my heavy heart, filled as it is with all the troubles and miseries I have endured since my Beltzi has been in Marienbad, I would need to write endlessly. But you don't even deserve, Chaim, a reply to your accusations and abuse. As surely as today is Tuesday all over the world, that's how totally wrong you are in accusing me. If you will read my letter carefully, you yourself will agree that you have not dealt with me as a good friend and an honest man would, but as an enemy and a vile person with a deceitful character. But let me go step by step and respond to your letter point by point.

Well, when it comes to your ranting at me like a fishwife, calling me names that even gossips on the Zselyaszne Bromme shy away from—I forgive you. I can imagine that most likely you got it in the neck from your Esther, poor thing, who is miserable. You had to let your rage out on me, though as God is my witness, I am innocent, may I be as innocent of evil. I swear to you that as I wish my Beltzi to be home soon in Warsaw, I did not show your Esther so much as a word of your letters to me or of my letters to you. May God help me if I can begin to understand how they got to your Esther. Quite the opposite—I was positive for a long time that it was *you* who had shown her *my* letters. How else would your Esther know that I had entrusted my Beltzi to your care in Marienbad so that you might help her out with an occasional loan and so on? Recently I went to your house to see how your Esther was doing and to convey to her regards from my Beltzi. She remarked, "Don't you have any close friends whom you could have appointed.as chaperon for your Beltzi other than my Chaim?" I immediately realized which way the wind was blowing but I managed to control my surprise and answered her, "I beg your pardon," I said, "but does asking your husband to lend her money make him into a chaperon?" She heard me out and said to me, "Do you know what, Reb Shlomo? Let's not talk about it anymore."

After such a conversation one would have to be, it seems to me, a complete idiot not to see that either you sent her the letters I wrote you or else you simply wrote her everything I had written to you about my Beltzi, though I don't understand for what purpose. Something else confirmed my suspicions that your Esther knew about my letters to you—when I was about to leave, your Esther called out to me, "Send my regards to your Beltzi and write her that when she comes back from Marienbad," she said, "through Berlin and goes to Wertheimer's, she should keep me in mind." Now how does your Esther know that my Beltzi was at Wertheimer's? Is she a prophetess or did a little bird from Marienbad carry the news to her?

But that's only the half of it. You wanted to humiliate me in your Esther's eyes so you told her things you shouldn't have told her under any circumstances. But never mind—what's done is done. But how deep does your hatred go that you had to call down another misfortune on my head? I'm talking about Berel Tchopnik. How does that swindler know that I wrote you about him and his wife, how after living in Warsaw twenty years not a soul knows who Tchopnik is or how this Tchopnik makes a living and other such tidbits? As carefully as I protect my own eyes from harm, so do I avoid saying so much as a word against this man, and I

128

can swear to you by all that is holy that, except to you, I have never said a bad word about him to anyone. He doesn't know, he says, what I have against him. He says that it seems to him we have never quarreled. And even though he still owes me a little money for rent (do you hear? A *little* money), we are, after all, he says, decent people and he hopes soon, with God's help, to settle with everyone and first of all with me because he considers me, in the first place, to be a fine, honest and good person with an easygoing character (do you hear, or not?) and in the second place, he says, we are, after all, kinsmen now.

"Kinsmen?" That really infuriated me. All right, an easygoing character and other such things—that I can tolerate, but when Berel Tchopnik claims kinship that can only mean he's sniffing around for a loan. It turns out that I was wrong. He actually *did* ask me for a loan but his main reason for coming was something else. "Why are you always saying bad things about me to everybody, so that all Marienbad should know, he says, that I am living for twenty years in Warsaw and don't pay rent and that I don't pay the butcher for meat or Hekselman for his catering?"

I don't have to tell you what his words did to me, Chaim. Although you're not a Kurlander, you should be able to figure it out yourself. I ask you, was it right for you to take my letters that I wrote you in strictest confidence and show them to Madam Tchopnik so that she should see what I wrote about her husband? And then you make up

129

other lies about me and falsely accuse *me* of showing your Esther the letters you wrote me and you heap abuse on my head, insulting me like a fishwife. No, Chaim, I won't insult you in return. I am not you. But I will tell you that you are a vile person with a depraved character and besides that, you're a little crazy and too short-tempered. There's nothing more to be said to you. "It's not enough to have brains," they say. "You have to know how to use them."

Your friend,
Shlomo K.

24.

Chan'tzi Mariomchik from the Nalevkis in Warsaw to her husband, Meyer Mariomchik, in Marienbad.

Dear Mark,

Your efforts are wasted. Your ingratiating letters in which you declare your love are worthless. I now know why you went abroad. I now know for whom you couldn't wait to go to Marienbad. It's all too late now, God have pity on me. Had I not been such a fool I would have figured it out sooner and not believed when a cheat like you tells me that the doctor prescribed a trip to Marienbad. I am enclosing here, Mark, a gift—a letter Shlomo Kurlander wrote to our Chaim and a letter our Chaim wrote to his friend Shlomo Kurlander. From these letters you will see how I know everything you have been up to in Marienbad. I see right before my eyes this loose woman whom Shlomo Kurlander brought home with him the third week after his wife's death, taking her—may he be cursed for it—with nothing more in her favor than her pretty face. Suddenly it all becomes clear to me. Suddenly I understand everything. Rest assured, Mark, that I will not stand in your way for long. Soon, soon I will untie your hands. Soon, soon, I will release you. The doctor came to see me twice today. He says that I have an infected liver and I must go to Marienbad if I'm to have any chance at all. But I will not go to Marienbad. Do you hear me, Mark? I would rather die than go to Marienbad and see how you are the plaything of dissolute women, how you race down to pick them up at the train station, how you bring them with you to your hotel, how you stroll about Marienbad with them and how you take them to the cinema, theaters and restaurants. That I should have lived to see this! May my parents rise up from their graves to see what has become of their youngest daughter, Chan'tzi! Why was I ever born if I had to meet you? A cruel death should have befallen your cousins, Velvel and his Yamayichke, who brought you here from Odessa! May the day be cursed on which I met you! My sister Esther was right to warn me time and time again to keep an

131

eye on you, to watch where you went and with
whom you spent your time in Warsaw. I knew you
were a skirt-chaser, but, who would have guessed
that it would be with Shlomo Kurlander's wife that
you would cook up this little scheme to run off
together to Marienbad? Was I blind? Was I
altogether oblivious? And what are your plans now,
Mark? I know your intentions, believe me, I know.
I know you inside out. You figure that this
Kurlander blockhead will find out about your
romance and will immediately divorce his Beltzi,
then you will get a divorce from me and the two of
you will marry and live happily ever after? Not on
your life! Shlomo will not divorce his wife and I will
not divorce you. I'd sooner die of my liver ailment
than willingly give you your freedom so you can be
yoked to that slut who sold herself for money to an
old scarecrow whose daughters are older than she is!
I can just picture your sorrow if I were suddenly to
die, God forbid, and your lamenting after I'm gone.
I don't know if you'd be able to survive it. But don't
start celebrating yet, Mark, because I'm not dying so
soon. First I'm going to make sure to torment you
good and proper. First you're going to have to suffer.
First I'll see you grow old and gray, unless, of
course, you decide to run off with that viper
somewhere, God knows where, to America. But you
haven't a kopek to get you there—not she, not you.
As you can see from the letters I'm enclosing, her
husband sends her money by the teaspoonful every
hour through our Chaim. And you? You're trying to
talk me into signing over my share of the

132

inheritance to Chaim for money so you can have more money for your womanizing? Not on your life! Instead I've decided to send for your Papasha from Odessa. Today or tomorrow he will be arriving. Let him find out what kind of a son he has and let him see what's become of me because of you in so short a time. I'm ashamed to show my face in public. Berel Tchopnik on the one hand and Velvel Yamayiker on the other go around wagging their tongues to everyone. They make sure to convey regards to me from you and from my brother-in-law Chaim, and from our Nalevkis ladies who have secluded themselves with you in Marienbad and are living the good life there. And as if I didn't have enough shame and heartache from you, you had to humiliate me further in front of strangers with that poem you sent me, "The Proud Bride." And I, fool that I am, listened to you and took "The Proud Bride" to the editors and there I was made a laughingstock. They were rolling on the floor with laughter and handed it back to me. "It's an old story—with a beard!" they said. I don't know what they meant by that, but I barely made it to the door. It was the last straw! Now I sit and impatiently wait for your Papasha to arrive. He will make you come back from Marienbad. You've spent enough time abroad for the cure—you're cured! Better come home, Mark, to your sick wife whom you may find on her deathbed.

Chan'tzi

133

25.

David Mariomchik from Odessa to his son,
Meyer Mariomchik, in Marienbad.

My dear son Mark,

I have just received two letters from Warsaw
which were enough to make me wish I were dead.
How you make my life miserable! I don't know what
you have against me. Two fine letters—either one
could drive a person to an early grave. One letter is
from a man from Warsaw who calls himself
Tchopnik. He writes me a whole *megillah* that he
has something on you, a packet of letters written by
you in Marienbad to two young Nalevkis women.
He wanted, he writes, to show them to your
Chan'tzi, but he felt sorry for her. He was afraid she
might, God forbid, have a heart attack right on the
spot. He writes that the poor thing is already sick
enough. He wants me to come to Warsaw so that he
can show me the letters and give me some advice on
what to do about them. I don't know who this
Tchopnik is but I have a feeling he's a blackmailer.
I don't know who these Nalevkis women are and I
don't know how you're mixed up with them in
Marienbad. The only thing I *do* know is that since
the day you were born you have been shortening my
life. Studying was not for you and business was

134

beyond you. You're only good at squandering money, dressing up and playing at billiards; otherwise you're good for nothing. I thought that once I married you off you would straighten out. I didn't stint on the marriage settlement and saw to it that you married into a respectable family of fine, well-off people. And in the end I see you are the same good-for-nothing you were as a boy in Odessa. I have no idea what goes through your head.

The other letter is from your Chan'tzi. She insists I come to Warsaw as soon as possible. She has, she writes, evidence that you've taken up with some young woman from Warsaw who is married to an old man and that you have run off with her to Marienbad. She says it's heading toward divorce, meaning that the old man wants a divorce and the wife is pressuring you to divorce Chan'tzi and marry her. God almighty! What I have to hear about you! So this is the *naches* I've lived to enjoy in my old age—to hear such marvelous news about you! Can you begin to appreciate my aggravation and anguish? I simply don't know what to do. If only your mother were alive now, I would send her to Warsaw or I myself would make the trip to see what's going on with you. But how can I leave the businesses and abandon the children just as they are about to start gymnasia? I don't know what to do first: Should I continue with my work on the Stock Exchange or should I look for a husband for Fanny, who is already of age, or should I put all that aside and go off to Warsaw to clear up the mess you've created? Consider it well, Mark. What will become of you?

It's high time you became a bit of a mensh. It's high time you stopped driving your father to his grave.

David Mariomchik

26.

Dr. Zeidener from Marienbad to his colleague in Kishinev.

Dear Colleague,

What the devil is keeping you in Kishinev? You have to be crazy to stay in Kishinev. Especially when there is a Marienbad on this earth. Listen to me—better come here to Marienbad and learn what life can be like. You'll relax a little, shake off that Kishinever dust, really see some sights and feel like a new man. I myself came here quite unintentionally. I was supposed to go to Ems or to Wiesbaden, but it so happened I was traveling from Vienna together with these salesmen from Lodz. Really, only one was a salesman, the other one was a druggist from Lumzhe. The whole way, we were engrossed in a game of Blackjack. They both played Blackjack so skillfully that soon I was desperate. I was convinced they were card sharks. From the start I was put off by their exchanging glances and by their talk. While they were making their bids they would speak in an odd way. I asked them. "What kind of language is that, boys?" They said, "It's Hebrew," and they went right on, *"Shishim v'shaysh"* . . . *"Moah v'chamishim"* . . . *"Sheli-sheli"* . . . in Hebrew. So I said to them, "Boys, if we are going to play Blackjack, you can speak any language you like but not Hebrew because I'm not a Zionist." They laughed and stopped speaking Hebrew but kept exchanging strange words. For instance, when one of them turned over the three face-down cards, he would say, "Praised be to Yusske the Mute, I just picked up three good cards—*zuhdik, lokritz, binyomin.*" Or: *"Mazel tov!* Itche-Meyer made a match with his Chemele and the Ludmerer maid." Now I know what those signals meant. *Zuhdik* is a red ten, *lokritz* the nine of clubs, *binyomin* the jack of spades, the *Ludmerer* maid the queen of diamonds, and so on. The trouble was that I figured it out much later, after those characters had cleaned me out. But in spite of that, we parted the best of friends. I haven't run into such warmhearted and fun-loving fellows in a long time. One of them told anecdotes and the other one sang songs—you could split your sides. As we were about to go our separate ways, we started a discussion about where I was going and where I was coming from. I said I was going to Ems. They said, "Fools go to Ems." I said, "I'm really not going to Ems, I'm going to Wiesbaden." They said, "Idiots go to Wiesbaden." I said, "So where do smart people go?" They said, "Smart people go to Marienbad." I said, "What's in Marienbad?" They said, "Warsaw

137

women." I said, "What's so great about that?" They
said, "Go and you'll see for yourself." In short, from
their talk and from the expression in their eyes, I
could tell that I had to go to Marienbad. I sent a
postcard off to my wife—thus and so—"don't write
me in Ems, write me in Marienbad, because on the
way I met two famous doctors, one of them a
specialist, and when they listened to my troubles
they said that the Kishinever doctors were cobblers.
Ems, they said, would be poison for me and
Wiesbaden would be my death. I needed, they said,
Marienbad, and the sooner the better" . . . and
so on.

And that, as you see, is how I came to be in
Marienbad and landed right in the Garden of Eden.
You probably want me to describe this paradise,
don't you? Not on your life! You're not too weak to
come here to see for yourself. What is there to do in
Kishinev? You should see these women! They aren't
women, I tell you, but peaches, little apples from
the Holy Land. Even in their wigs they look nicer
than the women in Odessa. And one is prettier than
the next. There's one little pomegranate, Beltzi they
call her. If you would catch an eyeful of this little
bonbon, you would go straight out of your mind. I'll
describe her to you: eyes—black cherries; cheeks—
red plums; teeth—white pearls; a little nose—
perfectly sculpted; neck—ivory; and her way of
dressing—it would knock your eyes out! Wouldn't
you know such a tender rosebud lives with an old
scarecrow? All the men are her slaves here. And
more than all of them, this Odesser dances around

her. Actually he is someone's brother-in-law from Warsaw. Mariomchik they call him—a braggart, a liar, who struts around like a cadet. I had a little run-in with him which almost led to a duel. Over nothing, but it's worth telling about.

In Marienbad there's this woman from Warsaw, Yamayichke they call her, who has three daughters with turned-up noses, getting on in years, who are looking for husbands. And since it isn't written on my forehead that I am married, they've taken me for a potential bridegroom, and the mother with the three daughters is spoiling me as if I were a beloved only son. The matchmaker is pestering me, all their friends consider me a suitor and are urging me on. More than all the others, one of these Warsaw women is working on me, a real fortune hunter who smokes little cigarettes and plays Preference with men—Madam Tchopnik is her name. This Tchopnik is driving me crazy. She says Yamayichke is as rich as Croesus, owns buildings in Warsaw, shops, estates, and so on. In a word, they're talking marriage. But I play dumb. A match is a match. What do I care? It so happened that this Odesser I was writing you about decided to publish a poem in Yiddish about Yamayichke's daughters. It was actually someone else's poem but he claimed it as his own. He had really plagiarized it and revised it a little. That was what almost led to the duel. His luck that he apologized and confessed before everyone that the poem wasn't his, that he had plagiarized it and revised it, and so on. In short, I'm living the good life here and certainly have no regrets that I am in Marienbad, not in Ems. Take my advice—come on out here. And tell Seriozha he should come to Marienbad too. Why are you wasting your time in that dusty old Kishinev? I hear you are occupying yourselves there with boring matters. I hear you are going to St. Petersburg with a delegation to protest the Patyeshna Boys' Regiment of the Czar. What for? Surely it would be fairer to allow Jewish children into the Patyeshna Regiment. But you're wasting your efforts. Our Volodke Purishkevitch, that anti-Semite of an editor, won't take it lying down. Write me what's doing at the Club. Who is winning and who is losing? I seldom play cards here. Here I spend my time flirting, and so far I'm doing very well—may it continue. Write me more often. But better yet, come. And not by yourself, but with Seriozha.

I kiss you.

> Your friend,
> Alfred Zeidener

27.

*Beltzi Kurlander from Marienbad to her
husband, Shlomo Kurlander, on the Nalevkis
in Warsaw.*

To my dear husband the learned Shlomo may his
light shine forever.

I must report to you that things are not going well
for me. If anything, I am even more nervous than
when I was in Warsaw. I am afraid my entire cure
and this stay in Marienbad are completely wasted.
And who is responsible if not you? As soon as I
arrived in Marienbad I was surrounded by so many
spies that I feared for my safety. I had no idea,
Shlomo, that before I came to Marienbad you had
already arranged for chaperons who would watch my
every step, who would keep track of where I went,
what I ate, when I drank and with whom I spoke.
How fitting was it of you, really, to complain to
your good friend that your wife is a spendthrift and
to ask him to enlighten me how poorly your business
is doing. And he, your "good friend," is so
considerate and refined that he takes the letters you
write him in the deepest of confidence and sends
them off to his Esther, and his Esther shows them to
her sister Chan'tzi, and Chan'tzi sends them to
Marienbad to her husband, Meyer'l Mariomchik, or,

141

as you call him, the Odesser Womanizer. The Odesser Womanizer is, if you want to know, far more refined than your "good friend," even if he *is* a womanizer. If not for him, I wouldn't have found out that you have spies in Marienbad and "good friends" who are prepared to use you for their own purposes and whom you believe in as in God. That being the case, I feel I must open your eyes to the real truth, Shlomo, so that you will know whom to trust and whom not to trust. I am sending you four letters from your "good friend" which were written to me soon after my arrival in Marienbad. Do read these notes—I'm sure you will enjoy them. I truly hope that afterward you will stop writing letters to him, won't entrust him with any more secrets and will stop pestering me about how I became involved with Odesser womanizers, Kishinever *shlimazels*, Lodzer dandies and other such good-for-nothings. Your confidant, Chaim Soroker, is, if you must know, a thousand times worse than his brother-in-law Mariomchik, even though he *is* a womanizer and has also annoyed me with *his* notes. I had to ask him not to dare write me such letters anymore or I would send them to his Chan'tzi. I'm sending them to you together with Chaim Soroker's letters so you will see what they are up to. You needn't employ any watchdogs, any spies or any protectors. With God's help, I can manage my own affairs. For instance, take those two *shlimazels* who were with me on the train from Berlin and who said goodbye to me at the Marienbad train station. Don't you think I ran into them here in Marienbad? Damn

142

them! They've since left, but at first they kept
showing up everywhere I went. Naturally I ignored
them, pretending I didn't recognize them. Do you
think they were bothered? No need to worry—they
didn't remain alone for very long. There are enough
older ladies and young wives here. There's a Broni
Loiferman and a Leah'tzi Broichshtul and a
Sherentzis and a Pekelis and other such pious
women who aren't particular—so long as there's a
young man and he wears pants, that makes him a
cavalier. And especially cavaliers like these two
pains in the neck who pretend to be single. The one
who kissed me and received a slap in return tells
anecdotes that are so funny you can split your sides
laughing, and the other one sings songs which
would put the Elyseum Theater to shame. You
would understand then why even Yamayichke
couldn't resist them and tried to charm them at the
mineral-water fountain where she introduced them
to her daughters. Only later on did she find out
from the matchmaker that these *shlimazels* were
married so she sent them packing. Ah, you will ask,
how come they didn't announce immediately that
they were married? And why didn't Mariomchik?
And why didn't your confidant, Chaim Soroker?
There is no doubt he is married and has children
almost as old as I am. How does it look for *him* to
write love notes? And to whom? To his good
friend's wife, who was entrusted into his
safekeeping! Believe me, Shlomo, I have wept
enough tears these days to fill an ocean. When I
think about it, why did I have to marry a wealthy

143

man? Wouldn't it have been better for me to marry
a man of my own station in life? Most likely I
wouldn't be in Marienbad now, God help me. If you
want to know the truth, Marienbad has been of no
use to me. On the contrary, since I've been here
I've lost more than two pounds. I asked the doctor
what to do for it and he said, "Eat more, walk less,
but most important, avoid getting upset and
aggravated." Some smart doctor! *That* I know
without *his* advice. I asked him if it would be better
for me to go to Frantzensbad and he said he had
nothing against that. If that's so, why shouldn't I
take a trip to Frantzensbad? They say that
Frantzensbad is not very far from here. It is a spa for
women only and is cheap, they say—half-price.
Broni Loiferman has been planning to go to
Frantzensbad and Leah'tzi Broichshtul too.
Sherentzis and Pekelis will most likely tag along too.
They imitate everything I do. Wherever I go they
follow, and whatever I wear appeals to them. If
their husbands, the two Itche-Meyers, could see how
their wives are carrying on they would dance for joy.
But I don't want to get involved in other people's
business. I have my own troubles and my own
burdens. Had I known what my cure would be like
in Marienbad I would never have come here for any
amount of money. I would never have listened to
my cousin and would better have gone to
Wiesbaden or to Ostend where at least there's the
ocean and one can go bathing. And what do we
have here? Here you can pass out from the heat,
here you are gossiped about by the Nalevkis

144

women—and because of whom? Because of you and your "good friends" in whom you believe as in a rabbi. After you've read his love notes to me, I hope you will realize what Chaim Soroker is really like and will stop writing him letters and considering him a confidant. If you wish to send me money, use the mail. About my uncles—don't you dare give them jobs because should anything go wrong later on, you will throw it up to me that I and my family are ruining you. Better to give them something toward their expenses and let them go to America. Then you'll know you're rid of them once and for all—and there's an end to it. Also I beg of you, please do not send any more instructions to your "good friend" and "confidant." Please make sure to see to everything in the house and tell Sheva-Rochel not to be in a hurry putting up cucumbers for winter while it's still so hot and cucumbers are so expensive. Write me if it's as hot in Warsaw as it is here, where you can't even dress properly to go out. May I soon see the day when I can leave here in good health for some other spa. This Marienbad and these Nalevkis cavaliers with their love notes have made me so miserable that, may God not punish me for saying this, I can't stand to look at them anymore.

From your wife,
Beltzi Kurlander

28.

Chaim Soroker from Marienbad to Beltzi
Kurlander in Marienbad.

Most respected Madam,

I am not one of those zealots who take upon
themselves God's work and who are ready to stand
guard over other men's wives and point out other
people's faults. Still I cannot restrain myself after
your cold reception of me last night. I must
enlighten you about that individual with whom I
met you yesterday. Perhaps you are not aware of
who he is. It's terribly unpleasant for me to say bad
things about one of my own—he is a brother-in-law
of mine—but *because* he is my brother-in-law, I
know him well. It is truly shameful for you to meet
with him, no less to be seen strolling in public with
him. Aside from the fact that he has an ugly
reputation going back to Odessa, he is also an
outrageous braggart and a dangerous scandalizer. I
write you these words only in order to protect your
good name and the honor of your husband, which is
as important to me as my own. I am doing my duty
only out of personal regard for you. You are coming
from Berlin and must be short of cash. I and my
purse are at your disposal.

A friend of your husband's,
C.S.

146

29.

Meyer Mariomchik from Marienbad to Beltzi
Kurlander in Marienbad.

My dear Madam Kurlander,

I see you are avoiding me and must therefore
reach you through the mail. I don't understand why
you are so standoffish. If it isn't agreeable for you to
meet me at the Jewish restaurant or at Café
Egerlander, why don't you come to the Café France,
where you were recently with your cousin, Madam
Tchopnik. It would be better if you could meet me
there alone today. I have to confide something to
you that is really interesting about my brother-in-
law, Chaim Soroker. By the way, what were you
two whispering about today at the fountain? Surely
you don't want to get involved with such an
unreliable person as my brother-in-law. What does
he have to talk to you about—the card games he
plays here day and night? Or about all the Nalevkis
love letters and affairs? I will expect you between
four and five.

Till we meet again,
M.M.

30.

Worthy Madam,

I cannot understand why you had to send a go-between. If you need money, you could have told me yourself yesterday at the restaurant. I told you as soon as you arrived in Marienbad that I and my purse are at your disposal always and at any time. But if it isn't convenient for you to come to me, I can come to you. For your sake I will spare no effort—first of all for the sake of your husband and second of all for your own sake. I would have sent the money to you with your go-between, but first of all, I would have to exchange Russian currency at the bank and second of all, I would prefer to put the money right in your hand as I wish to serve you in whatever way possible. Is that asking too much? At exactly eleven o'clock I will be at the fountain and if not then, at half past twelve at the Miramont. The Miramont would be better. There we would be able to talk, just the two of us. I have some very interesting information to pass on to you about your husband, and I also want to arrange for you to move to a more suitable hotel which would be cheaper and livelier. At my hotel you will find a crowd of

148

congenial people. We pass the time quite agreeably.
If there's nothing to do, we get up a card game.
Your husband himself isn't averse to playing cards.
How about you? So then, between eleven and
twelve-thirty.

With cordial regards,
Chaim S.

31.

*Meyer Mariomchik from Marienbad to Beltzi
Kurlander in Marienbad.*

Aren't you ashamed of yourself? I sat for two
hours waiting for you at the Café France hoping you
would come, but all in vain. How can a person be
so hard-hearted? You have apparently forgotten that
after we first met at the train station you told me
you didn't know how you could repay me. Now,
when I ask you for a small favor, you refuse me. I
give you my word of honor that if I saw you
together with my brother-in-law, Soroker, I would
act as if I didn't see you even though it would be
very painful for me. He is, after all, a close relative
of mine. But if you knew what I know about him,
you wouldn't meet with him anymore or so much as
respond to his greetings. You must think I am saying

this out of jealousy—I assure you that's not the case.
But the truth is I have in my possession evidence
that he insulted and maligned you, you and your
husband, every step of the way. A week from
Saturday I am making a trip to Eger. There are some
interesting things to see there. If you would join our
crowd, I will show you the evidence I just told you
about. Meanwhile, I remain your best friend.

M.D.M.

32.

Chaim Soroker from Marienbad to Beltzi
Kurlander in Marienbad.

A curse on these Nalevkis women. At home you
don't even see them except Saturday afternoon in
the Saxon Gardens. When they travel abroad, they
are everywhere all at once. I am not blaming you or
lecturing you. I only wonder why you did not show
up at the Miramont as I suggested because I had
something important to tell you, but instead you
went off with that wild bunch to Eger. Perhaps you
prefer to spend your time with them—may God help

you. Do you need more money? This evening I hope
to meet you on the Promenade.

Your best friend,
Chaim Soroker

33.

Meyer Mariomchik from Marienbad to Beltzi
Kurlander in Marienbad.

Dear Beltzi,

Please forgive my familiarity even though we are
not well acquainted with each other yet. It's a
practice of mine. If I truly respect someone, I must
call them by their first name and especially someone
like yourself who has enchanted me from the very
first. Tell me, *dushinka*, is it true what your cousin
Tchopnik told me about you, that you light candles
every Friday evening? I would believe it of Madam
Sherentzis or of Madam Pekelis because they are so
uneducated and simpleminded. I happen to know for
a fact that Sherentzis and Pekelis are also not quite
as religious as they appear to be in Warsaw on the
Nalevkis. There, in front of their Itche-Meyers, it's

fitting for them to bless the candles Friday evening.
I will prove it to you by taking them for a boat ride
on Shabbes—or my name isn't Mark Davidovitch!
Tell me frankly, *dushinka*, have the letters I showed
you convinced you what my brother-in-law is really
like? It's very unpleasant for me to have to
communicate with you by letter but what can we do
if they don't leave us alone for so much as a second?
How did you like the poem I wrote about
Yamayichke's daughters? Write me a few words, if
only to show you remember me. Don't be afraid.
Don't you trust me after all the evidence I've given
you?

Your Mark

34.

Chaim Soroker from Marienbad to Beltzi
Kurlander in Marienbad.

You are forcing me to tell you this straight out: it
is more enjoyable to spend time with you than with
all our Nalevkis women put together. Now are you
satisfied? Or would you prefer that I declare openly
what I have all but said and which you have already
surmised? Now I see why your husband trembles in
his boots. When one possesses such a treasure, one

152

does not sleep peacefully. You know I am not a person who wastes compliments, but one cannot walk away from the truth. If your face were matched by a softer heart, you could conquer the world. When will we see each other? How much more money do you need? I shall be waiting for you in the Jewish restaurant at the table where I always sit.

Your Chaim

35.

Meyer Mariomchik from Marienbad to Beltzi Kurlander in Marienbad.

Dushinka! Lyubenyu!

I am grateful to you for having clipped my brother-in-law's wings good and proper. Now he will know how to behave himself toward you. What do you say to this new development? Do we suffer from such a scarcity of escorts that the devil had to bring on a dentist from Kishinev? I don't see how one can tolerate such an uncultured boor. They are proposing a match between him and one of Yamayichke's daughters. What does she need him for? What right does he have to get involved with one of our Warsaw girls? I am told that he's very indignant about my poem, which everyone is now talking about. He's going all over Marienbad spreading rumors that the poem isn't mine and wants to challenge me to a duel over it. What an idiot! Even if it *isn't* mine, is that grounds for a duel? Generally I don't like to dirty my hands, otherwise I would write a poem about *him* that would be heard from here to Kishinev. For me it's easier to write a poem than to smoke a cigarette. When I was still in Odessa, I used to write no fewer than two dozen poems a day. And not only poems. I used to write articles, novels, comedies. Have you ever seen "Comedia Braka"? That's my work. Youskevitch also wrote a "Comedia Braka," but it's utterly worthless. Although I generally do not like to boast, you hardly are aware of all my talents. I hope that as you get better acquainted with me, you will change your opinion of me.

Your Mark

154

36.

Shlomo Kurlander from the Nalevkis in Warsaw to his wife, Beltzi Kurlander, in Marienbad.

To my dear wife Beltzi long may she live.

I received your letter and read over that fine packet of tender love notes from those brothers-in-law. What is there to say, my dear Beltzi? When married men, heads of families, have in mind such idle matters as running after other men's wives in these hard times, then, as you said, one cannot be sure of one's life. God almighty! Who was it that first thought up the idea of going abroad? Wouldn't it have been better that this "abroad" had been swallowed up in the earth like Korach or consumed by flames like Sodom before I had ever heard the word "abroad"? I can plainly see, Beltzi dearest, that this Marienbad is no laughing matter. It will be the ruin of me. If we weren't right in the middle of construction now—we are about to put the roofs on—I would put it all aside, sacrifice everything, let it all go to hell—and I would go straight to you in Marienbad to see for myself why it is that misfortune can't seem to evade you. How did this fate befall you? How come these wonders don't happen to *me*? How come no one sends *me* any flattering notes as they do to you? And why didn't you tell him right off then and there?—I'm referring to that vulgar potbelly, Chaim Soroker. Why did you have to wait till that Bessarabian glutton had to write me again and again? And what kind of sport is it to keep mailing letters to each other when you are all in the same city? In any case, when you see him on the street, stop and tell him once and for all, "Reb Chaim!" or "Mister Soroker! Tell me, what do you want? Are you studying letter writing in your old age? Don't you have anything better to do with your time? If not, here's a remedy—go knock your head against the wall!" You can be sure, Beltzi dearest, that those letters will boomerang. Though he says that the Kurlanders aren't worldly and though you write me off as old-fashioned, I will show you that the Bessarabians don't have as much between their ears as the Kurlanders have in the soles of their feet. I've worked out a plot and done a bit of mischief, which, I tell you, is priceless. All Nalevkis and all Warsaw will lap it up. As for that other scoundrel, Mariomchik, I took his letters right over to his Chan'tzi—let her get some pleasure out of them! Three times she fainted. They were barely able to revive her and had to call the doctor. And with Chaim Soroker's letters I pulled off a great stunt— you'll really enjoy this one. Since neither your name nor my name is mentioned in his letters, and there's plenty of space, I inserted the names of Broni Loiferman and Leah'tzi Broichshtul in the first two letters and Sherentzis and Pekelis in the other two. I then gave the letters to their husbands, each his own. Now let *them* suffer a little. Where is it written that *I* should be the only one to suffer? Let *them* stay up nights as I do. Let *them* feel the pains of the damned in their graves as I do and experience the bitter taste of a hell called Marienbad. For what he has done, that fat potbelly, Soroker, will get his just deserts, an eye for an eye, a blow for a blow, or, as the Russian peasants say, "Dig a grave for someone else and you will fall into it yourself." How do you like what I've accomplished? A brainstorm! And coming from a Kurlander too.

Now, Beltzi darling, let's leave these dogs and their love letters and talk a little about you, about your cure and about your new acquaintances in Marienbad. As if you didn't have enough trouble with Chaim Soroker and Meyer'l the Womanizer, a new *shlimazel* has latched onto you. I'm referring to that Kishinever dentist. Believe me, I know very well that there's nothing to it. So what's the problem, you'll ask? And I'll ask you in return, who needs it? What good does it do me for all of Marienbad and all of Warsaw to know that there's a Kishinever dentist and a Meyer'l Mariomchik who are tearing each other's hair out over Shlomo Kurlander's wife? There are no secrets, I tell you. You should know once and for all that nothing is said in Marienbad that is not heard in Warsaw. Should someone in Marienbad sneeze, someone in the Nalevkis will say "God bless you!" There is a saying, "What a person seeks he finds." If you travel abroad for the cure, then you have to devote yourself to the cure. You say you aren't happy in

Marienbad anymore and want a change of scenery?
Listen, I didn't like Marienbad from the very
beginning and nothing would make me happier than
to have you move on to another spa. So what's the
problem? I don't understand you, my dear Beltzi.
You yourself write me that from Marienbad to
Frantzensbad is a short hop, so hop over there. Why
waste time moaning and groaning? I am enclosing
some money for you and I beg you, don't disgrace
me; go immediately to Frantzensbad, but go without
escorts, without companions and without chaperons.
I will give you a bit of advice about what to do.
Wake up early in the morning when God Himself is
still asleep, get on a coach and start your cure all
over again, back to A–B–C, from the very
beginning. Forget there ever was a Marienbad on
this earth with cavaliers, Odessists, dentists and
other good-for-nothings. Do this for me this once
and you will see that I am a better friend than all
the others combined. I am not saying this to you,
because, heaven forbid, I don't trust you, or because
I have anything against them. What have they done
to me, really, and what do I care if they flutter
around you? Let them flutter around the Angel of
Death for all I care. It's only that I wish to protect
you from Jewish tongues. I don't want Yamayichke
to have something to gossip about and Meyer'l the
Womanizer to have something to scribble about,
and a Bessarabian porridge like Chaim Soroker to
have other men's wives to write love letters to—I'd
rather see him dead. Nowadays it's hard to know
who is a friend and who is an enemy. Berel

Tchopnik is an angel compared to Soroker. And I was such a fool and trusted Chaim Soroker and filled his ear with all my complaints about Tchopnik. He didn't waste a minute and showed it all to Madam Tchopnik, and now I'm really in hot water, may God help me! Berel Tchopnik came running to me in a dither and managed to talk me into giving him a loan which I'll never see again. Keep in mind, too, that Soroker swine isn't going to get away with anything. I just dispatched a letter to him such as he has never in his life received and rubbed his face in it so it will suffice unto the fifth generation! Don't worry, I didn't even mention his letters to you. I beg you, Beltzi sweetheart, write me how much money on my account you've taken from Chaim during this time, whether you signed any notes or whether he just gave you the money on your word. It would be a great service to teach that dog a lesson so that he would not howl anymore. Listen to me, my dearest Beltzi, leave that damned Marienbad, may it be cursed. But don't go with anyone else, go alone and write me how much longer you plan to spend abroad and when you plan to come home, God willing. Where are you thinking of going? You write "Frantzensbad" but according to what I have heard (there are no secrets in this world), you are going to Ostend. Write me, where is this Ostend located? And write me with whom you're going to Ostend. I assume, a friend. If you will be well and if God helps me and lets me live to see the day you return home healthy from the cure, I will vow to contribute toward your uncles' fares to emigrate to America because it's becoming impossible to put up with them. They are pulling me from all sides. The heat wave is awful, the expenses are getting worse, the paupers are so plentiful that there's no place to hide from them. Write me that you've received the money and, in God's name, less strolling and more curing, because your health is all that matters to me.

Your devoted husband,
Shlomo Kurlander

37.

Hirsh Loiferman from the Nalevkis in Warsaw to Chaim Soroker in Marienbad.

To the highly esteemed worthy and learned Mr. Chaim Soroker may his light shine forever.

I'm sure it has got to come as a big surprise to you to get a letter from me out of the blue seeing as how we never have had much to do with each other and really don't know each other, except that we go to the same synagogue on the High Holy Days. If you're surprised, believe me, I'm even more surprised. How come a man like you, a respected person, a reliable businessman and a father many times over should let himself carry on with another man's wife, to write her love letters and even offer her money? Who needs you and who needs your money? You must not realize that I might have as much cash as you. Don't take it personally, but I may be even richer than you because if we were to figure it out ruble for ruble, your money is all tied up in other peoples' pockets, and who knows what will happen a year from now if there is, God forbid, a financial crisis? I have, with God's help, ready cash because, as everyone knows, I did very well in the Warsaw lottery, and I can luckily maintain my wife not only in Marienbad but even in Paris. And second of all, my wife, thank God, is not the same article as those other wives like Madam Tchopnik or like Kurlander's little wife with whom your brother-in-law, the Odesser Womanizer Mariomchik, is carrying on, as I hear, such a business. Don't take it personally, but you write my wife such claptrap and such low-minded suggestions that should never enter the thoughts of a respectable man. At the same time, while you admit to her that you are not God's right hand, you find fault with her for spending time with such worthless characters like that brother-in-law of yours. And then after all that you have the nerve to tell my wife that you and your purse are at her disposal! Now, if I may say so, and don't take it personally, that is such a swinish thing to say that around here a person would get his bones broken for it. Then you have the gall to brag to my wife that we are fast friends and you have the nerve to sign

161

the letter "Your husband's friend." I ask you, and I mean you no harm, but since when did you become such a good friend of mine? Where were you during the times when I was down on my luck, let's hope it doesn't happen again? I used to feel really honored if you just answered my "Good Shabbes" and my "Good Yomtov." So I ask you, who is in such a great need of your friendship? I never needed nor did I ever ask for your credit, and now, with God's help, I certainly don't need any credit from you. Do you know what I'll tell you? Don't take it personally, but these letters of yours are fit for fine ladies like Madam Tchopnik and for other loose women but not for decent women from decent backgrounds.

That's all I have to say to you for now. The rest we can hash out, God willing, when you return home and we can deal with each other face to face. Meanwhile, be well and take care of yourself.

From me,
Tzvi Hirsh Loiferman

38.

Hirsh Loiferman from the Nalevkis in Warsaw to his wife, Broni Loiferman, in Marienbad.

Broni'shi,

What's going on? You keep writing me all the time to send you money and still more money when I have found out that you have in Marienbad such generous credit. *That* you didn't write about. It's a good thing I got hold of his letter to you, otherwise I would never have known how you're spending your time and what a good friend you've found there who puts himself and his purse at your disposal! Well, that he is a good friend of yours, you can easily figure out from his letter to you, but since when did *I* become such a good friend of *his* that he wants to defend my good name? Why didn't I hear of his friendship in those times when I was—may it never happen again—down and out and chasing all over Warsaw with my tongue hanging out, looking for a little cash? Now, all of a sudden, everyone wants to be my good friend. Naturally, Berel Tchopnik was first in line. Right after I won the lottery he came running, all smiles, and told me this great secret that he had always thought of me as a bright person, and sure enough I wound up giving him a small

163

loan. Even a man like Reb Velvel Yamayiker with his fine beard greets me with a big "Good morning!" All of a sudden I've become a hero in the bargain. It seems to me it's the same Hirsh Loiferman as before—but then not really the same. Even the newspapers made a to-do about the new rich guy from the Nalevkis. But let's put that aside. Tell me. Broni'shi, how do you let someone write such letters to you? How come you didn't send me his letter yourself? And how did you answer his letter? And write me if it's true that you've gotten to know his brother-in-law the Womanizer? And if it's true that you go strolling with Chaim on the street? And how come, judging from what he writes to you, after you gave him the cold shoulder, he still suggests that since you just came from Berlin you most likely need money and therefore he and his purse are always at your disposal!? I never heard of such *chutzpah*! Besides writing him an angry letter that he will never forget, I will show *his* letter to his wife—let her see it and let her know how her husband is taking the "cure" in Marienbad!

I beg you, Broni'shi, write me immediately all the details—what and when, because I won't overlook a thing like this. Also write me about your health and about everything else.

From me, your faithful husband,

Hirsh Loiferman

39.

*Kalman Broichshtul from the Nalevkis in
Warsaw to Chaim Soroker in Marienbad.*

To the worthy wealthy honored learned gentleman
Chaim Soroker may his light shine forever.

The purpose of this letter is to inquire of you to
be so kind as to explain quite honestly and frankly
without any deviousness or tricks: What kind of
business do you have with my wife that you are
writing her love letters? You invite her to meet you
at the fountain and at the Miramont to chat with
her tête-à-tête? You offer her money and you suggest
she move to your hotel for her own benefit? And
above all, what secrets do you have to tell her about
me???! In your letter to my wife you hint that I am
not averse to playing cards. If that's the secret you
have to disclose about me, you certainly haven't hit
the mark. All Warsaw knows I rarely play cards.
Occasionally I play a game of Buntshak or some
other game, but my life doesn't depend on it. I am
not Berel Tchopnik, I have other preoccupations. In
that case, what can you say against me to my wife?
And what can you possibly gain in doing so? A man
who writes such letters to another man's wife must
have important reasons and a serious purpose. The
fact that you haven't been getting along with your

165

wife lately—that is public knowledge. The Nalevkis is full of juicy gossip about it. Velvel Yamayiker told me some fine things about you—about you and your brother-in-law Mariomchik. People say the two of you are at the point of divorcing your wives. If that is so, I hope it will work out well for you. Now, only one thing remains: Why did you have to rush ahead and involve yourself so quickly with a second woman while she still has a husband, may he live to be a hundred and twenty? Or perhaps you know the secret that we too were once at the point of divorcing? But first of all, that concerns only my wife and myself, and second of all, you could at least have asked about it in a letter and not gone about it the way you have. By the way, since we've gotten to this point, I must tell you quite frankly that if I do decide to separate from my wife, I will only do it on two conditions: (1) under no circumstances can she have the children, and (2) the children must be provided for with a substantial sum of money in their names, deposited in the Gosudarstveneh Bank. You are a businessman and a clever person and you have apparently the same burden I do—a problem wife. But you must understand that there is a great difference between us. You are a capitalist and your children are financially secure, but I am not you. I give you my word of honor that I will not remarry a second time. Once burned is enough.

So, my friend, if you have serious intentions, answer me immediately—what and when and how. But if this is no more than a sport for you, as it is with your brother-in-law the Womanizer, who, according to what they write us from Marienbad, keeps chasing other men's wives and writing them love letters, then I don't understand how a man like you, a merchant and a father, can allow yourself to behave like that even though you are a rich man or even a millionaire. Obviously I will not tolerate this and a big scandal will come of it. In any case, I await your answer, one that is straightforward and responsible, without reservations or devices. I also just sent off a letter to my wife in Marienbad to write me whether it's true that she sent a messenger to you for money. And why didn't she ask me first? And what's this Miramont place you are inviting her to? And what secrets have you disclosed about me? Only when I've received her reply will I know for sure what I must do. In the meanwhile, it's all a big riddle to me.

I expect that if you have so much as a shred of decency, you will provide me with a satisfactory explanation for everything and will tell me exactly and expressly what you meant by your devious letter to my wife. What is your intent and your expectation? Most important, what kinds of secrets do you have to disclose about me, someone totally unknown to you?

Kalman Broichshtul

40.

Kalman Broichshtul from the Nalevkis in
Warsaw to his wife, Leah Broichshtul, in
Marienbad.

To my dear wife Leah'tzi long life to you.

It is not right, Leah'tzi, that I had to find out
about something so important involving such a
serious step third hand. It seems to me it would
have been far better for both of us had I found out
about it directly from you. I had already noticed
that you seemed to have something on your heart
but that you were trying your best to keep it from
me. Your sudden departure abroad, your insistence
on Marienbad—why did it *have* to be Marienbad?
Why not another spa?—and your infrequent and
brief letters to me lately—all these signs should have
alerted me. But how does the saying go? "The
husband is always the last to find out"? I would
never have believed and still don't believe that you
would sink so low as to allow yourself to send
someone for you to borrow money without my
knowledge from a man who seeks to undermine me
and blackens my name in order to attain his devious
ends. Even granting, as you have told me many
times, that I've made your life miserable (though

168

that's not altogether the whole truth—my life was made miserable by you), nevertheless it would have been far more honest had you written me thus and so, "Kalman dear, I wish to have my freedom because I'm sick and tired of living in constant deprivation. . ." and the like. I would have answered you in exactly the same way as I did before our first separation (do you remember?) with the Russian saying "Love can't be forced." So I say to you now, Leah'tzi, as a good and true friend and as the father of your children, that all doors are open to you. I will give you complete freedom but on one condition: Since you know the children are very precious to me and I will not be parted from them for all the money in the world, and, as he is a wealthy man (it would not hurt him if I had *half* his wealth), he should therefore see to it that first you and then our children are well provided for. Of myself, I'm not speaking. God will look after me without his help. You know that I've never been a demanding person and certainly am not that way now. So as long as I know you will be taken care of and that our children won't have to depend on a stepfather, that's all I ask. Another husband in my place would create a scandal. But I'm not a man who enjoys scandals. Therefore I am writing you calmly and with consideration. I also sent a letter off to him today and I am relying on his decency that he will give me a forthright explanation and this matter will be settled in an honorable way without a public scandal and my becoming a laughingstock.

Wishing you nothing but the best, your true
devoted husband who is in all ways your best friend,

Kalman Broichshtul

41.

*Itche-Meyer Sherentzis and Itche-Meyer
Pekelis from the Nalevkis in Warsaw to
Chaim Soroker in Marienbad. (Translated
from Hebrew)*

Peace be unto the highly respected distinguished
gentleman, the learned and enlightened Reb Chaim
Soroker—peace without end.

After thus greeting the distinguished gentleman
according to custom, we will take the liberty, with
his permission, to wish him a complete and speedy
recovery both in body and in worldly affairs. May
the Almighty bear him peacefully and speedily to
the serenity of his hearth and home and may he
know no more of illness or of pain and may this be
true for all of Israel from this day forth—Amen.

And now we must make a plea before the
eminence of our superior that he should incline his
ear to us and hearken to our cry, to the cry of the
blood of his brethren who call out from a far land
concerning the injustice that has been visited upon

170

them through no fault of their own. We said, "Let us but tell a thousandth part of our woe and heartache"—but the tongue wearies, the pen falters, and there are not enough sheets of paper on which to record it. We will be brief and attempt to provide only an echo of our outcry, violently erupting from the very walls of our hearts. Hear us out and God will hear you out.

We, the undersigned of this letter, are young men from Warsaw who have recently left their father's abode from which they were sent forth to earn a living by the sweat of their brows. And God blessed the doings of their hands and their labor bore fruit and their names grew great in the land, and, as is the custom of their brethren, the children of Israel, no sooner did the sun of success turn its face toward them and shine upon them than they began to squander that which they had gathered by the labor of their hands and money was as nothing in their eyes. Above all, they were prodigal with the wives of their youth and their wives began of a sudden to feel all sorts of pains in their limbs and they began to bow to the false gods of medicine who send forth these afflicted ones to the far ends of the earth seeking remedies for their wounds and more than anywhere else they are sent to that strange place of healing which is known by the name of Marienbad.

Let it be said that we observed all the commandments pertaining to Marienbad, every jot and tittle, all six hundred and thirteen commandments that are entailed therein. Not a cent was withheld or denied. Whatsoever the

doctors required we do, we did. We sent our
beloved wives to Marienbad and money was placed
in their purses for the journey and we said unto
them, "Go forth in gladness and good fortune to
that bountiful land of milk and honey and find there
your healing, only do not forget us and from time to
time let there be sent to us signs and other news of
your happiness and well-being until the joyous day
of your return to your nest and to your husbands,
the masters of your youth."

Thus did we speak to our beloved wives and bade
them farewell, and in peace they abandoned the
land of their birth and went to that land they had
chosen, meaning Marienbad, and vowed to send us
news from time to time. They kept their word and
wrote us letters about the state of their health and
of the waters which they continually draw forth
from the health-giving wells. But of a sudden all
word from them ceased. The post failed to deliver
any news from them. Impoverished and dried up
became the wellsprings of their letters until we went
mad and lived as in a nightmare. Suddenly our eyes
were opened up for us and all our questions were
answered. It was proven to us in black and white
just who was the guilty one and who was the
evildoer. Never in our lives would we have believed
it had we not seen with our own eyes and
recognized your handwriting and the handwriting of
your respected brother-in-law, penned on paper.
Most honorable and exalted sir! With the
smoothness of your talk you have ensnared them in

your net. Heapfuls of love have you poured into their laps and you apparently thought that no one would know of it, that not a soul would witness it. Oh, woe unto us! Who would have thought that in distant Marienbad there would exist a Gehenem awaiting them? Who would have believed that our pure and pious wives, who in their homes in Warsaw would have lived out their years without any knowledge of evil, should be so tempted? Who would have believed that in these times of Israel's woe, when all of Israel has been bound over to thieves, when Jewish blood is being shed like water in the streets, when swords are being sharpened against us on every side and storm clouds gather in our skies, that Jewish men, married men, fathers of children, would concern themselves with such unworthy matters, would deceive other men's wives somewhere abroad under the guise of healing and drinking life-giving waters and lead them from the path of righteousness to a place from which there is no return. Oh! Recoil, ye heavens! We had thought that only your respected brother-in-law, the husband of your wife's sister, whose name is known throughout the land as a dissolute person, who has cast off the yoke of piety and decency, was capable of committing such ugly deeds: writing letters to other men's wives, letters which he had delivered to our wives and which have fallen into our hands at great expense with the help of a person whose name we are obligated not to reveal. We thought that thus had the tragedy that cried out to heaven ended. But we concluded that we are *still* wanderers in the wilderness, that the real enemy lurked still in his hiding place and that enemy was no one else but you, respected and distinguished sir, you and no other. If the husband of your wife's sister, your respected brother-in-law, wrote nonsense and empty talk of thoughtless flirtations, then you, respected sir, had the audacity to tell our wives that for their sakes money would pour forth from your purse. Oh! Cursed be the hand that could write so! Cursed be the tongue whose smooth talk is as poison, whose honeyed words are as Gehenem!

All of this, we, the undersigned, most respected sir, have found necessary to pour into your lap, and we beg of you with every means of entreaty to take into account our honor, the honor of our wives as well as your own honor and to cease committing such unworthy deeds. We declare openly, most respected sir, that if you fail to hearken to our pleas and do not cease these secret indignities, then bitter will be your lot and you will earn your bitter wage and recompense many times over because there is still a God in heaven and there is a law and a judge in Israel!

We pray that you will not take offense at the brevity of this letter but we had little time. We hope you will grant an attentive ear to our words which are drenched in righteousness from a full heart and that you will not earn for yourself even greater disgrace. We close our letter and sign with much esteem and with a blessing from good friends

174

who wish you much happiness and wealth without end.

> These words from:
> Itzhak Meyer Sherentzis
> And these words from:
> Itzhak Meyer Pekelis

42.

Alexander Svirsky from Basel to Madam
Yamayiker in Marienbad.

Gracious Madam,

I have the great honor and privilege to inform you that I have arrived happily and safely in Basel for the Tenth Zionist Congress. As we had mutually agreed upon, I have engaged myself in my professional affairs with the utmost diligence to locate the suitable parties for your inestimable daughters and must hereupon announce, unfortunately, to my profound regret, that I have failed to locate these sought-for suitors because the greatest percentage of the participants at the Tenth Zionist Congress is composed of gentlemen who have long since been married. Regrettably, the unmarried ones are not to be found among the Zionists. The underlying reason for this is, obviously, that the Zionists, regrettably, marry early and are probably here for other underlying reasons, but the fact is undeniable that my journey to Basel has been completely fruitless and I am deeply pained by the expenses you have incurred for me. But I can justify myself insofar as your expenses have not been entirely to no avail because I have here in Basel been able to acquire information concerning your Kishinever party. To my greatest astonishment I have discovered that this Herr Zeidener *is* actually a very competent dentist who has an established practice in Kishinev, but regrettably, he is long married and has at home a very fine wife and children. What truly amazes me is how we could have permitted ourselves to be so deceived that the matter could have progressed to the point where he fell in love with all three of your inestimable daughters and that your three inestimable daughters responded in kind to him so that all of Marienbad thought of them as a proper match! But what *especially* irks me is the fact that this Herr Zeidener turns out to be a base conniver who borrowed some one thousand kronen from me as a short-term loan, and although I reminded him by telegraph twice that he should wire me these two thousand kronen posthaste to Basel, I remained without a reply and have to my greatest astonishment learned that Herr Zeidener has taken off for Ostend with Frau Kurlander, and that Herr Mariomchik, together with Frau Sherentzis and Frau Pekelis, has also taken off for Ostend, and this frivolous Herr Mariomchik still owes me two hundred kronen from a game of Okeh we once played together. But those two hundred kronen owed by Herr Mariomchik are not as grievous to me as the three thousand kronen owed by Herr Zeidener because the former is only a gambling debt and the latter is hard cash, money over which I sweated blood to earn—may he live to use it only for sickness, that scum! That bastard! Such hard-earned kronen as a matchmaker's fee—till you work out a match with Jews you can spit blood, and here comes some kind of dentist, a crazy man from Kishinev who has a wife and two children and passes himself off as an unmarried cavalier! It is disgusting that in our times, in the twentieth century, among civilized people, in a world of railroad trains, telegraph, telephone, electricity, phonograph, etcetera, etcetera, such a thing could happen! I am leaving from here directly to Ostend to collar that vile conniver and at the same time I will continue my search for respectable parties for your inestimable daughters.

With manifest esteem and with the best regards to your daughters,

I remain,
Alexander Svirsky

43.

Broni Loiferman from Marienbad to her husband, Hirsh Loiferman, on the Nalevkis in Warsaw.

To my husband the learned Hirsh may his light shine forever.

May all my enemies live through what I have been living through last night and the night before and this whole year. May that Yamayichke and that Tchopnichke know of good health as I know or even begin to understand *what* you are writing about and *who* you are writing about and to *whom* you are writing! This has to be a piece of gossip Yamayichke has cooked up with her Velvel Yamayiker. Or it's that Tchopnichke with her Berel Tchopnik who want to get out of repaying you a loan. Poor man, he really needs money badly because his wife has been losing heavily playing Okeh and has lost every cent she had. Now she's running to all our Warsaw friends trying to find an easy mark who will lend her some money for a short time. But there are no such fools in Marienbad. Most of them have already left, some for Frantzensbad, some for Ostend. Shlomo Kurlander's young wife is already in Ostend. Not alone. The Kishinever, whom I wrote you about, is also there. Where she is, there he is. Like magic.

178

But I must return to your letter. As I read it and reread it I almost go crazy! I can't begin to figure out what you are talking about. Who is this "he" you are writing me about who is such a good friend of mine and with whom I have credit? I don't have credit anywhere here even for as much as ten pfennigs. At the end of the week I receive a bill for the room and I have to pay. For the food at the kosher restaurant I pay meal by meal. So why are you throwing "credit" up to me? And what do you mean by saying you *saw* his letters to me? Whose letters? Except for your clever letters to me and except for the letters from my mother I haven't received a word from anyone. And to whom did I give the cold shoulder? And whose purse, as you say, is available to me? Really, Hirsh, you are talking as if you were confused or drunk. You are mixing together kasha and borsht and bringing up stories from the past that are over and done with. And then you ask me if it's true that I go strolling with him! If you are referring to the Odesser Womanizer, Meyer'l Mariomchik, well, if it weren't for Leah'tzi Broichshtul, I would have spit in his face a long time ago. She sticks up for him. She says it's a pity on him because he got carried away with Shlomo Kurlander's young wife. They were seeing a lot of each other when who should jump in but this Kishinever dentist who ran off with her to Ostend, apparently to get away from us because we would get in the way. But we figured, Leah'tzi Broichshtul and myself, that, God willing, next week after Shabbes, we would also take a little trip to Ostend because

179

here the season is almost over and there it is just
beginning. I am just waiting for the money you
mailed me and I beg you, Hirsh, please write me
exactly and in detail, not like a wild man, what and
whom you meant to reach with your letter, because
if my name weren't on it, I would think that either
it wasn't written to me at all or that you are, God
save us, out of your mind. And I must tell you the
truth; since you became lucky and won all that
money, you have actually become another person.
You go around night and day talking about your
winnings and you imagine that the whole world
envies you, that everyone is your enemy and
begrudges you your luck. And even your own wife
you don't trust, and you write such foolishness that
makes my head spin! When I receive the money,
and after I have arrived in Ostend, I will let you
know my address by telegram. Meanwhile, be well
and happy and please stop making a fool of yourself.
With best wishes,

> Your wife,
> Broni Loiferman

44.

*Leah'tzi Broichshtul from Marienbad to her
husband, Kalman Broichshtul, on the Nalevkis
in Warsaw.*

Highly Respected Herr Broichshtul,

Please forgive me, but after the kind of letter you
wrote me, I can address you by no other salutation
than "Highly respected Herr." I am not like you.
Only you can write a letter in which you address me
as "My dear wife, Leah'tzi." How can I be your
"dear wife" if I've done the things you've described?
I would just like to know who that man is who is
filling your ear with lies about me and from whom
I'm trying to borrow money. If you mean my Uncle
Yoneh from Petrikov, then first of all, it seems to
me I have a right to ask whatever I wish of him,
and second of all, I've never even raised the
question of borrowing money from him because I
know it would be useless, a waste of a stamp. Uncle
Yoneh has given us enough, more than enough;
even you can't deny that. I will be more than
satisfied if he keeps me in mind when making out
his will, but I doubt it. His children will most likely
prevent it. I simply don't know who you mean.
Maybe you mean Shlomo Kurlander? I've never
written to him about borrowing money nor would I.

Don't I remember that just before I left for abroad you approached him and he turned you down? But I *did* once borrow some money here from his Beltzi and I regret it. She is some article! She may yet do her husband in too. He really is a Kurlander "genius," but an honest man, and her carryings on here are shameful. But the devil take her, I'm positive she most likely started this gossip, either herself or through her husband, the genius, and *you* grabbed hold of it as just the pretext for a divorce. But I don't understand, why now of all times? And what did you find out about me which prompts you to say, "The husband is always the last to know"? You write that you are willingly granting me my freedom and I thank you very much for your generosity. Then you write that you wish to have provisions made for me and for the children. That's certainly very kind on your part. The question remains: *Who* should provide for us? And who is the "he" you are writing about who is supposed to be the provider? Still Uncle Yoneh? What does it have to do with him? If he wishes, he will provide; if he doesn't wish, he won't provide—what does that have to do with getting divorced? You write that another person in your place would make a scandal out of this. It seems to me that there can be no greater scandal than your letter. If I don't even have the right to correspond with my own uncle, then what's this world coming to?

If this is the situation, I have nothing more to do here. I don't have to continue with the cure. I had planned to travel to Ostend with Broni Loiferman.

But now I spit on all that and I am going instead to my Uncle Yoneh in Petrikov. I don't want to lay eyes on you anymore! You have reopened an old wound—you must want to do that—it's not the first time you've done it.

So goodbye. If you wish to write me, you can write me in Petrikov.

From me, your former friend, who doesn't deserve such letters,

Leah

45.

Chaim Soroker from Marienbad to Hirsh Loiferman on the Nalevkis in Warsaw.

To the affluent learned Tzvi Hirsh Loiferman,

I have received your letter. It pains me greatly but I must tell you that I pity you your winnings because your winnings, it appears, have driven you out of your mind. You have unfortunately taken leave of your senses. You write that you are richer than I am. It is quite possible. I am not about to give an accounting comparing my income with yours and I believe you when you say you can maintain your wife even in Paris. May God help you and grant you your wish. But I ask you, what has that to do with me? How could I ever have written letters to your wife when I don't even know her? She neither requested money of me nor did I offer her any. And never did I boast of my friendship with you as I have never considered myself a friend of yours. There has to be a terrible mistake. You have surely missed the mark and most surely meant to take my brother-in-law Mariomchik to task. He and your wife *are*, in fact, thick as thieves. As I have heard, he is at this moment with her in Ostend. You can write letters to them there boasting of your wealth and leave me alone because as I have always been, so I now remain,

Your unknown friend, who hopes you will soon return to your right mind,

Chaim Soroker

46.

Chaim Soroker from Marienbad to Kalman Broichshtul on the Nalevkis in Warsaw.

My unknown friend,

I don't know how to respond to your letter. I can only give you this piece of advice—take the time to

184

visit a good doctor who can diagnose your peculiar state of mind, but so that it won't be altogether boring to you, look up Hirsh Loiferman, the one who struck it rich and has come down with the same ailment as you. What other conclusion can I reach after you write me that I have tried to inveigle your wife into moving into my hotel *for her own benefit* and that I revealed to her that you play Okeh? Whether you play Okeh or play Buntshak—*that* I do not know. But that you are not in your right mind is perfectly plain from your letter. You write that you've known for a long time that I haven't been getting along with my wife and you submit as a witness Reb Velvel Yamayiker. It is possible that Reb Velvel Yamayiker knows better than I how I get along with my wife but when you say that I know you are at the point of divorcing *your* wife—well, now you are speaking, if you will pardon me, like a true madman. Not only do I know nothing about such secrets between you and your wife, but I know neither your wife nor you, and the two of you interest me so little that for all I care you could have gotten divorced even before you met. But I do agree with you on one point: You should not, as you write, marry a second time. A person like yourself should not have gotten married the first time because it's a pity on your wife, although I don't know her.

You ask me to write you honestly and frankly what my intention is in inviting your wife to the Miramont—so I tell you plainly and openly and without any deviousness or devices, as you requested, that either your wife is, you should pardon me, a liar and a falsifier or, as I said at the start of my letter, you are not in your right mind. I would suppose the latter is more likely.

As you see, I have given you a satisfactory explanation for everything. Only one thing remains—to wish *you* a speedy recovery.

Chaim Soroker

47.

Berel Tchopnik from the Nalevkis in Warsaw to his wife, Chava'le Tchopnik, in Marienbad.

Dear Eva,

You must forgive me that the money was so late in coming the last few times.

Lately it's become very difficult in Warsaw to lay one's hands on a hundred or a fifty, simply impossible. I had to make a trip to Lodz, where I finally was able to work out a few deals with great difficulty, and that's another reason I didn't respond to your letters so quickly.

Unfortunately I could do nothing with the love notes to the two Itche-Meyers' wives. With one of them, Sherentzis, I might have been able to work something out, but he fears a scandal; he's worried that it will hurt his credit. But the younger one, Pekelis, is really a simpleton. He himself had spread it all over the Nalevkis, telling everyone in secret so that by the time I got to Madam Soroker with the letters, it turns out that she and her sister Chan'tzi, Mariomchik's wife, already knew Meyer'l's letters by heart. It didn't seem advisable to start in with them, and in addition, I happened to drop in at a time when Madam Soroker was in the middle of a crisis in which her Chaim had gotten mixed up with Shlomo Kurlander and Loiferman and Broichshtul— all of the Nalevkis. I am simply amazed that you haven't heard about it. The whole story is basically very simple. Chaim Soroker, not having anything to keep him busy in Marienbad, simply became jealous of his brother-in-law and also took to writing love notes to Nalevkis women—to Beltzi Kurlander, to Broni Loiferman, to Leah'tzi Broichshtul, and to Sherentzis and Pekelis—he didn't leave anyone out. No one knows how it happened, but these letters fell into their husbands' hands and it's turned into a three-ring circus and all of Warsaw is boiling over with it. And in the midst of all this here comes a telegram from Madam Yamayiker from Marienbad saying that our Nalevkis wives have suddenly disappeared, gone off to Ostend, and with them, Chaim Soroker and Meyer'l Mariomchik. It's simply a novel! And when does this telegram arrive? Just after the morning Yamayichke had announced to her family the good news of her daughter's

187

engagement and requested that Herr Yamayiker come to Marienbad. Velvel Yamayiker is already on his way there but that's not important. The most important thing is that Frau Soroker has unfortunately fallen gravely ill from aggravation and has taken to her bed, they say, in serious condition. And Loiferman is chasing around like a maniac, vowing that as soon as Chaim Soroker comes home he will slap him in the middle of the Nalevkis. Not on the Nalevkis but in the face! And Broichshtul now has a pretext for getting a divorce from his Madam or weaseling money out of her rich uncle in Petrikov. In short, here on the Nalevkis it is simply lively, simply merry. Do write me when you plan to come home and whether the money I sent you is enough. If it isn't I will send you more if I can. Somehow, God will provide. I send you my love.

From me, your most devoted
Bernard

48.

*Chaim Soroker from Marienbad to Itche-
Meyer Sherentzis and Itche-Meyer Pekelis on
the Nalevkis in Warsaw.*

My dear friends Sherentzis and Pekelis,

It is a pity that I do not possess the fluency of the
holy tongue as you do and cannot reply to your
eloquent letter in similar eloquent language. But as I
am forced to speak in the mother tongue, I will
allow myself to use blunt language and tell you that
you are, I must beg your pardons, a pair of fools,
Nalevker asses who should both be given straw to
chew. If God did grant you the gift of two such
pretty wives whom you quake in your shoes worrying
over, then you should always make sure to walk
behind them, as you do on Shabbes afternoons
while they go strolling in the Saxon Gardens. Or
cage them up on the Nalevkis as one would cage up
chickens before a holiday and give them food and
water and so forth. Who on earth told you to let
them go free, especially in Marienbad? Do you think
there aren't enough women here without them? Or
do you really believe that I have nothing better to
do than write love letters and mash notes to your
wives? Rest assured, my dear Itche-Meyers, that I
have, all in all, spoken no more than half a word

189

with your wives since I've been here and since I've been born! All in all, I've seen them perhaps two or three times at the fountain with many others like them who loiter there so much of the time that it has become tiresome, don't be offended, to look at them. I know the type. I don't mean your wives in particular, I mean all the Nalevkis women who, no sooner do they leave their Itche-Meyers in Warsaw to go abroad, than they yearn to taste all worldly pleasures, but only so long as no one sees it or knows of it, even they themselves. Talking with a strange man or even looking at one is a big event for them. On the Nalevkis where you are, they do not have the opportunity to do that. I can tell you upon my word of honor that I make every effort, whenever possible, to avoid such encounters, which lead nowhere except to ugly talk and gossip. I flee from such women who at home light the Shabbes candles and here cast off their wigs. They are fair game for my brother-in-law Mariomchik, but not for me, and I do not know who had the gall to point his finger at me, telling you I am the one who is writing love letters and mash notes. I do not waste my time on such nonsense. But even worse, how could you accuse me of having promised your wives to, as you say, "make money pour forth from my purse for their sakes"? I am not one of those profligates and could not care less about you and your wives. If someone pointed the finger at my brother-in-law, "the husband of my wife's sister," as you call him, then you should have contacted him or my wife's sister, not me, who have nothing to do with them. You may in fact be, as you say, very respectable young men and innocent Itche-Meyers, but you are not obliged to be complete idiots and do not have to threaten me with the Law and with punishment, not in this world and not in the next.

Your unknown friend who advises you to be careful with eloquent language,

Chaim Soroker

49.

Chava'le Tchopnik from Ostend to her husband, Berel Tchopnik, on the Nalevkis in Warsaw.

My dear Bernard,

It is very unpleasant for me to write still another time that you must get me money to leave this place because all our hopes are dashed, the dam has broken, and there is a big scandal which will shock you when you hear the details! Just try to imagine this comedy—did I say comedy? A tragedy, a bloody tragedy. But let me tell you exactly what happened from beginning to end. It's a tale from *The Thousand and One Nights.*

As you know, the Yamayichke asked me to help

her out with the Kishinever match and promised
me, in addition to the commission I would earn, the
bonus of a fine personal gift. So I did as she desired,
really putting my mind to it, and it worked out. The
matter moved ahead smoothly—not that it
happened overnight. I was quite distressed by Beltzi,
as I wrote you before, because the bridegroom, my
Kishinever dentist, got himself seriously worked up
over our Shlomo Kurlander's little wife and nearly
came to blows with Meyer'l Mariomchik over her in
the middle of Marienbad. In brief, after much
trouble, considerable pain and several intrigues, I
finally managed to convince the Kishinever dentist
to declare his love for Yamayichke's oldest daughter.
The Yamayichke threw her arms around me and
kissed me for joy. She immediately sent off a
telegram to Velvel Yamayiker to come here for the
betrothal party. For me it was a success all around.
That great international matchmaker, the impresario
behind the whole match, Svirsky, had left for Basel,
so I was the only one left on the scene. But of
course, there's still a Beltzi to deal with. Suddenly
our Kurlander's little wife had the notion to take off
then and there for Ostend. She didn't even say
goodbye to anyone, not so much as a by-your-leave.
Well, she left and that was that. May nothing worse
happen. But then my bridegroom, the Kishinever
dentist, has some second thoughts, picks himself up
and also goes off to Ostend. How do I know this?
From Meyer'l Mariomchik. I am down at the
fountain where I run into Mariomchik, who is
terribly upset and is ready to say his goodbyes to me.

192

"Be well," I say. "Have a nice trip. Where are you going?" "To Ostend." "Why suddenly to Ostend?" I say. He says, "Everyone is going to Ostend." I say, "Who is everyone?" He says, "First—Madam Kurlander, second—Madam Loiferman, third—your bridegroom, the Kishinever dentist. . . ." As soon as he said those words, I didn't want to hear any more and went right off to the Yamayichke. It turns out she doesn't have any inkling of this yet. The two of us go directly to the hotel to check on the Kishinever bridegroom and they tell us he's left. Where to? They don't know. Throwing her arms around my neck, the Yamayichke says pleadingly, "My dear soul, my dear heart, *lyubenyu!*" Would I please go directly to Ostend, she will take care of my expenses—she will do anything! And she takes out a hundred kronen. "Here you are. Go. Be sure to send me a telegram. If you need more, I will send you more." What could I do? It was a pity on the poor woman! I took the money but before I knew it, here a penny, there a penny, there was nothing left of it. And I was already up to my ears in debt! What can I do? If that were only the worst thing, it still wouldn't be so bad. Now you'll really hear something.

I'm sitting in my hotel, ashamed to be seen by the Yamayichke and I am thinking—where can I get some money? An idea pops into my head. Chaim Soroker! Between you and me, he really is a pig of a man, but I have a way to deal with him. I will tell him that I'm going home to Warsaw and will send regards to his Esther from Marienbad. Knowing him,

193

he will certainly want to know what kind of regards it will be. I've told him plenty of times that I know he is infatuated with Beltzi and that he lends her money on her husband's account and other such things—I'm not ashamed to let him know these things. In short, I call his hotel and ask them to get Herr Soroker for me but I am told that Herr Soroker has "this morning left for Ostend." God in heaven! What's going on here? I throw on my cape and am about to run out not knowing where when I am informed that a lady is calling on me. What's this now, a lady? Probably the Yamayichke. I wanted to sink into the earth. I proceed to ask, "What kind of a lady?" They tell me, "A young woman." "A young woman? Send her in!" The door opens and in comes a lady—a beauty! A young one—peaches and cream, dressed like a princess, all glowing and sparkling. "You are," she says, "Madam Tchopnik from Warsaw?" "I am," I say, "Madam Tchopnik from Warsaw, and who are you?" "I am," she says, "Madam Zeidener from Kishinev." "I am pleased to meet you," I say, "Sit down, Madam Zeidener from Kishinev. What brings you here?" She heaves a sigh and says to me, "They told me you are acquainted with my husband." "Who is your husband?" She blushes and says to me, "My husband is Zeidener from Kishinev." "You mean the dentist?" "Yes, he is a dentist."

What happened from that point on I don't have to tell you. I started to tremble as if in a fever. How can I describe the pity I felt for this young woman? In half an hour the two of us became as close as sisters, even closer than sisters. And without giving it a moment's thought, I packed my things—Madam Zeidener lent me money to settle my account—and both of us took off for Ostend. Arriving in Ostend, we took rooms in a hotel, washed up, dressed nicely, hired a hansom and made the rounds of the hotels asking for a gentleman with the name Zeidener and a woman with the name Kurlander. A waste of time! They were not to be found—not Zeidener, not Kurlander. We rushed to take a look at the list of guests at the spa—not even a hint of a Zeidener or of a Kurlander! What to do now? For me to have lived through that night, I must be stronger than iron. The poor young woman almost went out of her mind. I came to her rescue and called in a doctor—she was nearly at the point of committing suicide several times. Then I had the bright idea that she should send a telegram home to Kishinev letting them know she is ill, just in case anyone might be traveling to Ostend from there. Why do *I* need an additional burden on myself? Don't you think a telegram arrived from there and "special delivery" into the bargain. And it was from Zeidener himself, saying he is in Kishinev and he is asking her to come home! When we received that telegram we didn't know whether to laugh or cry. We decided to send another wire to Kishinev asking if it were true that he, the dentist Zeidener, was in Kishinev and when did he arrive and did he come alone or with anyone else? He answers us that it's true, he *is* in Kishinev, he just arrived yesterday from Marienbad all alone and he doesn't understand why he is being asked these questions and how come his wife is in Ostend? That was when I first realized that it was Mariomchik, the Odesser Womanizer, who had led me astray, who had thought up this cock-and-bull story. Now only one thing remains to be cleared up—since the story about Ostend is an invented one and since the dentist Zeidener is in Kishinev, then what's happened with Beltzi and where did she go? And what's become of her? That's why I wired you, "Where is Beltzi and where are the rest of the Warsaw women?" You apparently didn't understand and answered me, "What is all this about Beltzi and what are you doing in Ostend?" My answer to that reply was these few words, "Send money." Do you want to know why? Because I didn't have enough money for a longer message and still don't have any. Madam Zeidener, as soon as she received the good news that her worries were over, picked herself up and went home, promising she would write en route and after she arrived at home. But did she do so? Forget it! Luckily I'm staying at a hotel with full pension and they haven't asked me to pay yet. But surely they'll be asking to be paid soon. I don't know what I'll do then. I've written to the Yamayichke in Marienbad already, even telegraphed her. Does a wall answer? I tried to write to Chaim Soroker in Marienbad but my letter was returned marked that the addressee had gone to Ostend. Again to Ostend? I am going crazy. I go back to look over the spa register and try to find the name of Soroker. I take a look—in one hotel is written the name "Solomon Kurlander, salesman from Warsaw" and in another hotel, "Alexander Svirsky from Marienbad." Now there's a surprise! I run first to one hotel, then to the second one, and only then do I find out that indeed Shlomo Kurlander and the marriage broker, Svirsky, have stayed there for a few days. Why have they been there? I am now altogether confused and don't know what is going on.

So I've written you all there is to know, dear Bernard, the whole tale from *The Thousand and One Nights*. Now be so kind and write me, first of all, what's happened to Beltzi and the other Nalevkis women? And what was Shlomo Kurlander doing here? And what's happened to Chaim Soroker and Meyer'l Mariomchik? Where are they now and where are the Yamayichke and her daughters? Is the marriage broker, Svirsky, with them in Warsaw? I must know because this Svirsky made a promise to me, giving me his word of honor that whatever match would be worked out with Yamayichke, I would have a share. But most important, get some money and send it to me and, God help us, send it as soon as possible so I won't have to remain here, God forbid, over the holidays. It's getting close to the High Holy Days and I refuse to eat anything unkosher. I will have to find a kosher restaurant, and there you can't eat meals on credit. And I will want to go to *shul* and these Germans make you pay for a seat in advance. I will most likely have a white hen prepared for the Yom Kippur ritual—and I don't have a groschen to my name! What I could pawn, I've already pawned. I didn't want to cause you any grief. I wouldn't be writing you now if all these misfortunes hadn't happened all at the same time.

Be well, my dear Bernard. May God write our names in the Book of Life. And a year like this one, with this going abroad that I've had, may it never happen again, God in heaven!

Your devoted wife,
Chava

50.

Frau Zeidener, Ostend, to Herr Zeidener, Kishinev.

ARRIVED YESTERDAY MARIENBAD OSTEND.
ALFRED NOT HERE. FELL ILL. WIRE BELLEVUE.

REBECCA ZEIDENER

51.

Chava'le Tchopnik, Ostend, to Pearl Yamayiker, Marienbad.

ZEIDENER NOT OSTEND. WIRE.

EVA TCHOPNIK

52.

Herr Zeidener, Kishinev, to Frau Zeidener, Ostend.

(URGENT)
SAFELY ARRIVED KISHINEV. SURPRISED. DIDN'T FIND REBECCA HOME. COME IMMEDIATELY. WIRE.

ALFRED ZEIDENER

53.

Chava Tchopnik, Ostend, to Pearl Yamayiker,
Marienbad.

ZEIDENER KISHINEV. LETTER FOLLOWS.

TCHOPNIK

54.

Shlomo Kurlander, Warsaw, to Beltzi Kurlander,
Marienbad.

NO LETTER LONG TIME. WHERE WRITE?
MARIENBAD? FRANTZENSBAD? OSTEND?
ANXIOUSLY. WIRE.

SOLOMON

55.

Chava'le Tchopnik, Ostend, to Pearl Yamayiker, Marienbad.

WIRE OSTEND BELLEVUE. WHERE BELTZI
SOROKER MARIOMCHIK LOIFERMAN
SHERENTZIS PEKELIS? OSTEND NOT.

EVA TCHOPNIK

56.

Frau Zeidener, Ostend, to Herr Zeidener, Kishinev.

WIRE IF TRUE ALFRED KISHINEV. ALONE OR
WITH SOMEONE?

REBECCA

57.

Herr Zeidener, Kishinev, to Frau Zeidener, Ostend.

YESTERDAY ARRIVED ALONE. DON'T
UNDERSTAND WHY ASKING. WHY WENT
OSTEND? LEAVE IMMEDIATELY. WAITING
IMPATIENTLY. WIRE URGENT.

ALFRED

58.

Esther Soroker, Warsaw, to Chaim Soroker,
Marienbad.

NO LETTERS LONG TIME. IMPATIENT. WIRE.
ESTHER·

59.

*Shlomo Kurlander, Warsaw, to Beltzi Kurlander,
Ostend.*

YAMAYICHKE WIRES YOU IN OSTEND. WIRE
ADDRESS TO SEND MONEY. ANXIOUSLY.

SOLOMON

60.

*Chan'tzi Mariomchik, Warsaw, to David Mariomchik,
Odessa.*

WIRE FROM MARIENBAD MARK RAN OFF WITH
NALEVKIS WOMEN OSTEND. COME
IMMEDIATELY WARSAW. WIRE.

ANNA

61.

Esther Soroker, Warsaw, to David Mariomchik, Odessa.

CHAN'TZI GRAVELY ILL. COME IMMEDIATELY
WARSAW. WIRE.

ESTHER

62.

Frau Zeidener, Ostend, to Herr Zeidener, Kishinev.

TRAVELING EXPRESS TRAIN. KISSES.

REBECCA

63.

Eva Tchopnik, Ostend, to Berel Tchopnik, Warsaw.

WIRE OSTEND BELLEVUE. WHERE BELTZI
SOROKER MARIOMCHIK OTHER NALEVKIS
WOMEN?

EVA

64.

*Velvel Yamayiker, Warsaw, to Pearl Yamayiker,
Marienbad.*

RECEIVED LETTER. APPROVE KISHINEVER
MATCH. WIRED MAZEL TOV. COMING EXPRESS
MARIENBAD.

VOLF

65.

David Mariomchik, Odessa, to Chan'tzi Mariomchik, Warsaw.

ARRIVING EXPRESS WARSAW. WIRE.

DAVID

66.

Alexander Svirsky, Ostend, to Pearl Yamayiker, Marienbad.

ARRIVED OSTEND. DIDN'T FIND ZEIDENER KURLANDER. PERHAPS MARIENBAD? WIRE POSTE RESTANTE.

SVIRSKY

67.

Pearl Yamayiker, Marienbad, to Alexander Svirsky, Ostend.

ZEIDENER KISHINEV. KURLANDER VANISHED. WIRE.

PEARL YAMAYIKER

68.

Berel Tchopnik, Warsaw, to Chava Tchopnik, Ostend.

WHY WORRYING BELTZI? WHY NALEVKIS WOMEN? WHY IN OSTEND? WIRE.

BERNARD

69.

Madam Tchopnik, Ostend, to Berel Tchopnik, Warsaw.

SEND MONEY IMMEDIATELY. LETTER FOLLOWS.
FIRST OPPORTUNITY. WIRE.

EVA

70.

Pearl Yamayiker, Marienbad, to Velvel Yamayiker, Warsaw.

MATCH OFF. KISHINEVER MARRIED. DON'T
COME MARIENBAD. BELTZI BRONI SOROKER
MARIOMCHIK VANISHED. PLAN TRAVEL
WARSAW.

PEARL

71.

Chaim Soroker, Marienbad, to Esther Soroker, Warsaw.

CURE FINISHED. TRAVELING BERLIN WARSAW.
WIRE BERLIN SAVOY. BE WELL. KISSES.

CHAIM

72.

Shlomo Kurlander, Warsaw, to Chaim Soroker, Marienbad.

ANSWER COLLECT. HAVE PITY. WIRE WHERE
BELTZI? MARIENBAD OR OSTEND?

SOLOMON KURLANDER

73.

Shlomo Kurlander, Warsaw, to Pearl Yamayiker, Marienbad.

ANSWER COLLECT. WIRE IF TRUE BELTZI
SOROKER MARIOMCHIK VANISHED? THEIR
ADDRESS? HAVE PITY. PREPARED GO
MARIENBAD OSTEND.

SOLOMON KURLANDER

74.

Beltzi Kurlander, Alexandrova, to Shlomo Kurlander, Warsaw.

TRAVELED MARIENBAD BERLIN. CATASTROPHE.
THINGS CONFISCATED BORDER. COME WITH
MONEY OR SEND THREE HUNDRED
ALEXANDROVA. WIRE.

BELTZI

75.

Esther Soroker, Warsaw, to Chaim Soroker, Berlin.

WHY RUSH WARSAW? BELTZI BRONI NOT HERE
YET. SHERENTZIS PEKELIS ALSO NOT. LEAH'TZI
BROICHSHTUL PETRIKOV. FATHER-IN-LAW
MARIOMCHIK ARRIVED CHAN'TZI DIVORCE.
YOU CAN SAME. MAJOR DECISION.

ESTHER

76.

Beltzi Kurlander, Alexandrova, to Shlomo Kurlander,
Warsaw.

YESTERDAY WIRED COME ALEXANDROVA OR
SEND THREE HUNDRED. WHY NO ANSWER?
WIRE.

BELTZI

77.

Pearl Yamayiker, Marienbad, to Velvel Yamayiker, Warsaw.

YESTERDAY WIRED DON'T COME MARIENBAD. MATCH OFF. BELTZI BRONI SOROKER MARIOMCHIK NOT IN OSTEND. I CHILDREN TRAVELING BERLIN WARSAW. WIRE.

PEARL

78.

Itzhak Meyer Sherentzis and Itzhak Meyer Pekelis, Warsaw to Pearl Yamayiker, Marienbad.

ANSWER COLLECT. TCHOPNIK WIRES WHERE SHERENTZIS PEKELIS. WIRE IF SHEINTZI KREINTZI NOT IN MARIENBAD. IN OSTEND? ANXIOUSLY.

SHERENTZIS PEKELIS

79.

Beltzi Kurlander, Alexandrova, to Shlomo Kurlander, Warsaw.

WHY NOT COMING ALEXANDROVA? NOT
SENDING THREE HUNDRED? EVERYTHING LOST.
GREAT HUMILIATION. ANXIOUSLY. WIRE.

BELTZI

80.

Madam Sherentzis and Madam Pekelis, Marienbad, to Sherentzis and Pekelis, Warsaw.

TRAVELING WARSAW. STOP BERLIN
WERTHEIMER. REGARDS.

SHEINTZI KREINTZI

81.

Alexander Svirsky, Kishinev, to Pearl Yamayiker, Marienbad.

MONEY GONE. WASTED EXPENSES. BIG
SCANDAL. PROPOSE LETTERS THREE PARTIES
YOUR THREE DAUGHTERS. WIRE IF COME
MARIENBAD OR RENDEZVOUS VIENNA HOTEL
NATIONAL? FIRST CLASS MATERIAL. ONE
DOCTOR TWO LAWYERS. BEST REFERENCES.

SVIRSKY

82.

Kalman Broichshtul, Warsaw, to Leah'tzi Broichshtul, Petrikov.

DISCOVERED KURLANDER FORGED SOROKER
LETTERS TO BELTZI. SOROKER PLANS
PROSECUTE KURLANDER. I WITNESS.
KURLANDER OSTEND SEEKING BELTZI. BEG
FORGIVENESS. COME WARSAW. KISSES.

KALMAN

214

83.

Broni Loiferman, Berlin, to Hirsh Loiferman, Warsaw.

TELEGRAM MARIENBAD ARRIVED HERE. THIRD
DAY BERLIN. TOMORROW WARSAW. BE
ALEXANDROVA. WIRE WHY LEAH'TZI PETRIKOV.
WHERE BELTZI? KISSES.

BRONI

84.

Berel Tchopnik, Warsaw, to Chava Tchopnik, Ostend.

LETTER RECEIVED. EVERYTHING CLEAR. MONEY
SENT. BELTZI ARRIVED. THREE DAYS
ALEXANDROVA BORDER SCANDAL. KURLANDER
ABROAD SEEKING BELTZI. SOROKER ARRIVED
FOUND ESTHER GRAVELY ILL. WANTS FILE
AGAINST KURLANDER FORGED LETTERS.
LOIFERMAN BROICHSHTUL ALSO. SHERENTZIS
PEKELIS WITNESSES. BELTZI BESIDE HERSELF.

215

BEGS MAKE PEACE. I DEMAND THREE
THOUSAND. WILL WIPE HIM OUT.
MARIOMCHIK DIVORCING. LEAH'TZI PETRIKOV
RICH UNCLE. YAMAYIKER MARIENBAD
BETROTHAL PARTY. YAMAYICHKE DAUGHTERS
WARSAW. SVIRSKY GONE. COME WARSAW.
WIRE. KISSES.

BERNARD

85.

*Shlomo Kurlander, Marienbad, to Esther Soroker,
Warsaw.*

MARIENBAD FOUND NO ONE. GOING
OSTEND. WIRE POSTE RESTANTE.

KURLANDER

86.

Hirsh Loiferman, Warsaw, to Pearl Yamayiker, Marienbad.

YOU WIRE WIFE VANISHED? WIFE WIRED BERLIN COMING WARSAW. FORGERIES. COMPLAINTS PROSECUTED.

LOIFERMAN

87.

Velvel Yamayiker, Marienbad, to Velvel Yamayiker, Warsaw.

ARRIVED MARIENBAD BETROTHAL PARTY. FOUND NO ONE. SAID WENT WARSAW. WIRE WHERE PEARL? CHILDREN? ANXIOUSLY.

VOLF

217

88.

Pearl Yamayiker, Warsaw, to Velvel Yamayiker, Marienbad.

WHY GO MARIENBAD? WIRED DON'T GO.
BRIDEGROOM WIFE TWO CHILDREN. RETURN
WARSAW. WIRE.

PEARL

89.

Shlomo Kurlander, Ostend, to Esther Soroker, Warsaw.

OSTEND ALSO NO ONE. PLAN RETURN
MARIENBAD. THEN KISHINEV. WIRE.

KURLANDER

90.

Velvel Yamayiker, Marienbad, to Pearl Yamayiker, Warsaw.

TELEGRAM RECEIVED. DON'T UNDERSTAND.
WHY BRIDEGROOM, KISHINEV? WHY TWO
CHILDREN? WHERE THIRD? WHO BACK IN
WARSAW? WIRE.

VOLF

91.

Pearl Yamayiker, Warsaw, to Velvel Yamayiker, Marienbad.

WIRED MATCH OFF. BRIDEGROOM KISHINEV
MARRIED. DON'T GO MARIENBAD. YOU WENT
MARIENBAD. DIDN'T WIRE. WASTED EXPENSES.
WIRED RETURNING WARSAW. I CHILDREN
WARSAW. WIRE.

PEARL

92.

Velvel Yamayiker, Marienbad, to Pearl Yamayiker, Warsaw.

YOU WIRE I DIDN'T WIRE? WIRED TWICE. WIRED MAZEL TOV. WIRED DEPARTURE. WHY NOT WIRED IMMEDIATELY BRIDEGROOM KISHINEV MARRIED? WHY NOT WAIT MARIENBAD? WHERE MATCHMAKER? WHERE TCHOPNIK? WHERE BELTZI? WIRE.

VOLF

93.

Pearl Yamayiker, Warsaw, to Velvel Yamayiker, Marienbad.

HOW LONG THIS WIRING? WIRED BELTZI ARRIVED. KURLANDER MARIENBAD OSTEND SEEKING BELTZI. MARIOMCHIK DIVORCED. LOIFERMAN MAKING SCANDAL, WANTS SLAP KURLANDER. ESTHER CRITICAL. SOROKER PROSECUTE KURLANDER. BROICHSHTUL, SHERENTZIS, PEKELIS WITNESSES. TCHOPNIK SETTLED. SVIRSKY WIRES KISHINEV THREE

MATCHES. ENOUGH WIRES. COME HOME
IMMEDIATELY. WIRE.

PEARL

94.

*Shlomo Kurlander, Marienbad, to Shlomo Kurlander,
Warsaw.*

YAMAYICHKE WIRED BELTZI SUDDENLY
VANISHED. WAS MARIENBAD, WAS OSTEND.
RETURNED MARIENBAD SEEKING BELTZI. WIRED
EVERYONE. NO ONE WIRED BACK. WHO AT
HOME? WIRE WHERE BELTZI? SHOULD GO
KISHINEV? WIRE URGENT.

SOLOMON KURLANDER

95.

*Beltzi Kurlander, Warsaw, to Shlomo Kurlander,
Marienbad.*

YAMAYICHKE LIED. TRAVELED MARIENBAD
BERLIN WARSAW. DETAINED BORDER

ALEXANDROVA. WIRED THREE TIMES SEND
MONEY. EVERYTHING LOST. JUST ARRIVED.
WHAT HAVE YOU DONE? BECAUSE OF YOU
BROICHSHTUL DIVORCING. MARIOMCHIK
ALREADY DIVORCED. ESTHER SERIOUSLY
ILL. SOROKER THREATENS CRIMINAL
PROCEEDINGS. LOIFERMAN, BROICHSHTUL,
SHERENTZIS, PEKELIS WITNESSES. TCHOPNIK
SWEARS TO WIPE YOU OUT. DEMANDS THREE
THOUSAND. WIRE.

BELTZI

96.

*Shlomo Kurlander, Marienbad, to Beltzi Kurlander,
Warsaw.*

THOUSAND THANKS. GREAT NEWS. HELL WITH
SOROKER. SPIT ON LOIFERMAN. THREE
THOUSAND PLAGUES TCHOPNIK. LEAVING
EXPRESS BERLIN WARSAW. KISSES.

SOLOMON